HIS PERFECT PREY

FRATERNITAS

LEE SAVINO

To all the readers who crave a nice primal fuck with a psycho masked man... Start running.

The rules of the Hunt: The prey will have a ten minute head start to run.

At the signal, the hunter will enter the woods. **The Hunt has begun.**

If the prey isn't captured before midnight, she gets $10,000.
If she makes it until dawn, she gets $100,000.
But **if the hunter catches her, she's his for the night.**
There's one final, secret rule only the hunter knows: what the hunter catches, he keeps. His prey will become his elita, his chosen. **She will belong to him. Forever.**
Let the hunt begin...

Tropes: mafia brotherhood, secret society, primal play, dark romance, Little Red Riding Hood and the Big, Bad Wolf

Content warnings:
Primal play, non-consent/reluctance, BDSM, sex work, abduction/seduction, violence and murder (on page), narcotics addiction (past), erotic scenes.

Check out the His Perfect Prey playlist here: https://geni.us/ HisPreyplaylist

*Check out A Mafia Christmas Story here: https://geni.us/
HisPreyfreebie*

1

J*aeger*

BILLIONAIRE ISLAND IS an oasis outside of the city. The richest of the rich own vacation homes here. And it's home to the Lodge, a private club set on several hundred acres of wooded land. The elite come here to party, gamble at the private tables, and partake in the bacchanal delights offered in the BDSM dungeon on the lower floors.

I stand at the bar with a drink in my hand, studying its amber depths. At six feet three and over two hundred pounds of pure muscle, I don't fit in with the glitzy and glamorous set. Unlike the trust fund bros and businessmen with soft hands, I wasn't born into privilege. I was born on the street. I've spent my life surviving on the knife's edge of danger. This soft life doesn't suit me. I came to the Lodge to clear my head, but not even the burn of expensive whiskey was enough to sate the monster prowling inside me.

The beast wants to feed.

I need to get some pussy. It's been far too long, and the Lodge is full of beautiful women. The waitresses are in short skirts, and the club submissives are in barely-there-body-suits. Not to mention the socialites and heiresses here in designer dresses, seeking a walk and ride on the wild side. I can feel them looking at me. I could crook my finger and snare any of them. But that doesn't interest me at all.

I prefer a brutal chase. I need the thrill of the hunt to sate the beast.

I'm looking around for the pretty redhead I saw a few days ago at Inferno, the bar our brotherhood runs in the city. Sometimes, the girls who work at Inferno also pick up shifts here at the Lodge.

I haven't been able to get her out of my mind—curly red hair, tight curves, and a few freckles showing through her heavy makeup. She's just my type. My dream girl brought to life. When I first spotted her, I thought I was asleep. She was so stunning, it was like the gods created her from my fantasies.

But she's not here.

I down my whiskey and rap my finger against the bar for another.

"Happy birthday, Jaeger." Sebastian St. James emerges from the shadows. He invited me here, so I should've been expecting him. Only years of training allow me to hide the fact that he's snuck up on me.

"St. James." I turn to face him. St. James is in his usual gray suit. From silk tie to silver cufflinks, every tailored inch of him looks the part of a successful, well-bred business-man. Only those of us who know him well know he's dangerous. "How did you know it was my birthday?"

St. James doesn't answer. He sips his drink, calm under

my intense scrutiny. He's my blood brother, but I still tread carefully around him.

When you live on the outskirts of society the way I have, you catalog threats. All my life, I've been surrounded by dangerous men. I've just made myself a bigger threat than the rest. But my instincts recognize that St. James is on another level. He's as subtle as a snake in the grass and just as deadly, and all the men he's destroyed never saw it coming.

"Right. You know everything." This isn't the day my twin brother and I were actually born. It's a day we chose for ourselves. This is the day we were freed from hell and reborn.

But St. James probably knows that, too.

"I have a gift for you," he says.

I snort. "Do you think I just turned seven? Birthday gifts are for kids." Not that I know from experience. My upbringing didn't afford any childish celebrations.

"I think you'll like this gift." He snaps his fingers, and a cute blonde dressed as a cigar girl sashays over. St. James selects two cigars from her tray and heads out of the Lodge and onto the massive wooden deck overlooking the thick forest. I follow him. He's head of Fraternitas, second in command only to the man called the Devil. I follow him because I've sworn to do so.

But I'm also intrigued.

St. James takes our cigars across the deck to the far railing. I lean on it and look out at the acres of wilderness. You'd never know a city of nine million was a few miles away. The only sounds are the rustling leaves, the hum of insects, and the hoots and howls of night creatures. It's peaceful and wild.

It soothes the beast.

A match flares, and St. James hands me my cigar.

Now that he's piqued my curiosity, the bastard's going to make me beg. "So what is it? My gift?"

"I spoke to Damien." He means the Devil. Head of Fraternitas. "He and I agreed you deserve a reward for the sacrifices you've made."

He's referring to the last six months that I spent on a mission for Fraternitas. The one that left my hands stained in so much blood I'll never be able to scrub them clean. "Everything I do, I do for the brotherhood. To uphold my vow."

"We know that. You've proven your loyalty many times. And thus, you've earned a reward." He flicks ash over the side of the rail.

Somewhere beneath us, an alarm sounds. I tense as a door under the deck bangs open.

A figure races out onto the lawn. A woman, bare-legged, wearing a white dress that glows in the moonlight.

My whole body is on high alert, my muscles tightening, ready to give chase.

My twin and I have excellent night vision. It's one of the reasons we're so deadly in the dark. My gift allows me to pick out the details of the runner. She's got a wealth of curly hair tumbling down her back, and her pale legs flash as she pelts across the lawn, away from the Lodge.

I track her until she disappears into the tree line, every instinct in me telling me to run after her.

St. James smokes his cigar, watching me with amusement. I'm gripping the railing hard enough to get splinters.

"Who is she?" I growl.

"A waitress. She typically works at Inferno, but I assigned her other duties tonight." Godsdamn St. James. He noticed me watching the redhead and lured both of us here. He has something planned.

"What duties?"

"She's yours for the night. If you can catch her." His gray eyes glitter in the moonlight. St. James likes edge play. That's why he owns multiple BDSM clubs, including the Lodge.

And if he knows everything, he knows there's nothing I like better than a wild, primal hunt.

"She signed a contract and everything and is being well paid to run from you in the woods. She gets a bonus if she eludes you past midnight. More if she makes it until dawn." He gives me a satisfied look, the closest thing he has to a smile. "I doubt it'll take you that long to hunt her down."

"You mean..." The beast is roaring in my chest. My chest is swelling, my lungs preparing to pump like bellows and get me ready to run after her. My prey.

"Welcome to the Hunt. You have free reign of the property until dawn. And when you catch her, she's all yours." He pulls out a black mask—a simple hood with eye holes and a white skull painted on the front. It's what I wear for ritual executions. He hands it to me and nods to the stairs to the left of us that lead down to the lawn. "I told her you'd give her a ten-minute head start."

ELODIE

I DASH BETWEEN THE TREES, racing with my arms outstretched to push through the branches, but briars scratch at my bare limbs and face.

A full moon shines brightly overhead, helping me see

my way through this thicket, but I know it also illuminates the dress I'm wearing. The white is the opposite of camouflage. I might as well be spotlit on a stage.

The jerk who hired me made me put on this white dress. Luckily, it's the end of summer, and the nights aren't that cold. But I'm barefoot, too. It's obvious I'm supposed to fulfill some specific fantasy. This is the Hunt, and I'm the poor, helpless prey. Half-naked, dressed like a virgin, and ready for sacrifice.

Whatever. As long as I get paid.

Waitressing isn't enough to get me and my sister out of the mess her ex created. I need the thousand dollars Mr. St. James offered me to take this gig. He also dangled a bonus if I avoid getting caught before midnight. He wants me incentivized to give the patron a real hunt.

If I last until midnight, I get ten thousand dollars. But if I make it until morning, he'll give me a hundred thousand in unmarked bills.

That's the goal. A thousand dollars will help our problems. Ten thousand will fix them.

One hundred thousand will change our lives. I have to keep from getting caught.

I strip off the white dress as I run. I rip it into pieces and hang one strip on a low branch, where it hovers in the air, suspended like a ghost.

I weave through the towering oaks, leaving scraps of my dress on the branches of the smaller elms and holly trees. Red herrings to throw the hunter off my scent.

But now I'm naked. And my pale skin is a beacon in the night.

The woods end, and I race through the long grasses of the lawn. My feet slide into mud, and I flail to keep from falling. The black glimmer in front of me must be a small pond.

Behind me, back at the Lodge, there's a blast of a horn. The long, low note sends chills up my arms. That must be the signal St. James told me about. He promised me that I'd know when the hunter headed out after me.

I'm running out of time.

The Hunt has begun.

*J*AEGER

I jog down the stairs and head for the forest. The only sign of St. James is the burning end of his cigar. I don't give a damn that he's watching. My whole focus is on the sweet scent hovering in the air—the scent of my prey.

I strip off my shirt, and my skin prickles in the cool air. It's summer, but the night is starting to have a bite to it.

I was born feral. From day one, my twin and I fought for survival like weeds growing through a crack on the sidewalk. It wasn't until I said my vows and joined Fraternitas that I got to experience the world beyond the concrete jungle. The first time I came out here and heard the chorus of crickets and breathed the fresh air, I was home.

St. James and the Devil were visionaries, even when they were young. They figured out how to turn the petty crimes of a gang of street rats into a profitable gambling and smuggling enterprise and expanded into real estate before we were old enough to own land. Fraternitas owns almost all of Billionaire Island, including the vast acreage where we built the Lodge. There's a privacy fence around our land, but I'd have to jog miles to reach it.

Plenty of wilderness for me to hunt.

I tug on the executioner's hood. Now, I look like what I am: a killer. A beast bred to lurk in the wilderness on the outskirts of society. I'm lucky Fratenitas has a need for my monstrous urges; otherwise, I'd have been put down like a dog.

This is why I've never claimed a woman. No one should have to suffer the savagery of my possession.

But now, I have a sacrifice that's been offered up on a platter, and I'll be damned if I don't take it.

"Run, run, Little Red," I hum to myself, picking up my pace until I'm jogging through trees. "Here comes the Big, Bad Wolf."

~

ELODIE

THE HUNTER IS CLOSE, stalking through the woods. He's wearing heavy boots and snapping twigs underfoot with little care for being stealthy. He even hums a little. He's having a blast hunting a human for sport.

The closer he gets, the more noise he makes, but the sounds are drowned out by the pounding of my heart. Waitressing gave me strong legs, but I'm not a runner. That's why I opted to hide.

I press myself against a thick tree trunk. I took the time to smear mud on my skin so I'm not glowing in the dark. It was disgusting, but I needed camouflage. I also piled leaves over the mud on my legs. Hopefully, it will keep the bugs away from me.

I fight to still my breathing and try to become one with the tree bark. But I can't resist peeking to see if I can get a glimpse of the hunter.

That's my first mistake. He steps into the moonlight, and

my lungs seize. He's massive, with tattoos etched on his burly arms and a hood painted with a skull covering his face. He's the stuff of nightmares.

My stomach does a slow, lazy flip. This guy is way bigger than I thought he'd be. This is no ordinary client, and he's not just a club patron who's rich enough to pay for his fantasies.

He has to be one of *them*. One of the Fraternitas. The biggest, baddest gang in the city. They rule the criminal underworld. No one knows what it takes to join their ranks, but there are rumors. Blood rituals, executions. Fight clubs to weed out the weak. Only the strongest survive to join the brotherhood.

If I had known I was going to be hunted by a criminal monster, I wouldn't have signed the contract. There's no telling what depraved things he'll do if he catches me.

Too late now. I'm being hunted, and something tells me I can't just stand up and wave a white flag. This isn't over until he catches me or I win.

I have to win.

Now that I've seen the threat, I can't tear my eyes away. I study him for clues. For all his size, he lopes easily around the pond, his movements as fluid as a panther's. Even as my insides cramp with fear, heat stirs deep in my core. His muscles are beautiful in the moonlight.

I'm doing my best not to move or breathe, but something alerts him. He stops and raises his head, a predator scenting his prey.

Then he swivels and faces the part of the woods I'm hiding in. It's impossible, but I have the strangest sense he's looking right at me.

JAEGER

THE NIGHT IS BEAUTIFUL. The moon overhead might as well be a floodlight on the meadow. I skirt the pond, noting a few streaks of mud on the grass. My prey was here.

I can feel her watching me.

Even though I was born and bred in the city, I've honed my hunting skills. I know the little redhead is naked. She stripped off her shift and tore it into pieces, leaving them scattered around the forest like little white flags of surrender, shivering in the breeze.

I clench one in my fist. It still bears her warmth, her scent. She's not far away. She opted to hide, not run.

I take my sweet time strolling to the next copse. Once I'm there, I make as much noise as I can. I push through the brush, careless of where I step, and kick leaves and branches out of my way.

If she won't run, I'll scare her until her primal instincts take over and she makes a mistake.

"I know you're here, little red," I call. "I can smell you. You're not the first prey I've hunted."

I pause, listening hard. I can't be sure, but I sense someone breathing nearby. "Do you know what my enemies call me?" I turn in a slow circle, scanning the trees. "Nothing. They don't know who I am at all, not even after I've slit their throats." There's a dark shape up in the canopy, but it looks like a squirrel's nest. These oaks don't have enough low branches for my prey to climb. "But my brothers call me the Wolf." I keep walking, weaving through the trees. I see a drift of leaves that might be big enough to hide a person and head over and kick it, but it's nothing but leaves.

There's a bit of movement out of the corner of my eye. Instead of turning toward it, I continue on.

The night is young, and I want to take my time. I want this hunt to last.

~

ELODIE

I CLENCH my teeth so hard they ache. The hunter walks right past me, carrying on a one-sided conversation. He's a bigger jerk than St. James. I add him to my mental People I Want to Kill list and try not to dwell on how sexy his deep voice is.

I must be a freak because my body reads my fear as excitement. Every boom of my heart makes my pussy throb. Wetness trickles down my leg.

This guy wants to fuck me like an animal on the cold, hard ground, and I'm turned on? I don't understand myself.

His voice grows distant. I hold my breath until I no longer hear him crashing through the underbrush. The sounds recede until I'm left with the silence of the forest. But there's not really silence. There are strange creaks and cracks and rustling sounds. I don't want to think about what sort of nocturnal creatures are creeping around these woods. I can only hope they leave me alone.

There's a whine near my ear, and I flinch. The mosquitoes have found me. And the temperature has fallen. I'd be warm enough if I were wearing clothes, but now I'm shivering.

Another whine and I slap my arm where the bug lands. The mud has dried and started flaking off. I roll my lips to keep in a hysterical giggle. If he does find me, he might think I'm too disgusting to touch.

I wait a few long moments. It has to be close to midnight, right? The window of my normal bedtime has passed, leaving me wide-eyed and wired.

And hungry. And freezing.

Maybe I can head back to the Lodge. Sneak in and hide somewhere warm. It's breaking the rules, but if I produce myself at dawn, covered in mud and leaves, everyone will assume I did my part.

Slowly, carefully, I rise to my feet. I'm lost in the shadows of the huge tree. There's no one around.

He's gone.

I slip from shadow to shadow. I won't take the shortcut across the meadow. I'll keep to the woods.

I've gone ten steps when a deep voice at my back murmurs. "There you are."

2

E *lodie*

I DART across the grass with the hunter on my heels.

Crap, crap, crappity crap!

He tricked me. He made it sound like he stomped away from my hiding place when he either snuck back around to lie in wait or never left.

I don't look back. I run in the direction of the Lodge, my legs pumping as fast as they can go.

I was stupid. My whole plan was stupid. What was I thinking, trying to outwit a seasoned hunter? He's an apex predator, and I'm at the bottom of the food chain.

Now I'm naked and flying across a stretch of lawn around the pond. My boobs are bouncing like mad. Not to mention my butt, belly, and thighs. There's a reason I'm not a runner. Too much bouncing.

Meanwhile, he's built like a warrior, able to run and fight

for hours. My lungs are shrieking for air after a hundred-yard dash.

If he catches me, he could do anything. The contract allows him full access to my body, and for a chance at life-changing money, I signed on the dotted line. When I was in the warmth and safety of the Lodge, it made sense. But now that I'm deep in the dark woods, I'm wondering what the hell I've gotten myself into. Out here, a contract is just a piece of paper. It means nothing. There's no logic, just adrenaline. Things could easily get out of control.

He could hurt me, kill me. Choke me out and do terrible things to my unconscious body, with only the trees as witnesses.

Out here in the woods, there's no one to help me. No one to hear me scream.

I'm not just running to escape so I can get paid. I'm running for my life.

Fear gives my feet wings as I sprint through the trees.

Gotta get ahead, gotta hide. I'm about to slow down when he appears on my right, a skull-faced specter.

"Boo."

I veer left. This isn't fair. He's playing with me. Taunting me. His legs are so long that he's jogging lazily and still able to keep pace.

"Run, run, little red."

That's it. My heart's about to burst. His taunting pushes me past fear into anger.

Enough running like a rabbit. I've spent my whole life being chewed up and spit out by those bigger and badder than me. This night has finally pushed me over the edge.

I have to stand my ground. If I die, I die. At least I'll die knowing I stood my ground.

I halt in a small clearing and whirl around. He's melted

into the shadows where I can't see him, but I can feel him watching me.

"Come on then!" I call, raising my arms in challenge. "Come get me."

He appears, and I jump back. He looks deadly in his executioner's hood. The shifting shadows make his tattoos writhe like snakes on his chest.

I'm panting and shaking, and he's barely out of breath.

"You're giving up?" His voice is dark and velvety, stroking between my legs.

"Screw you," I fire back. He thinks this is all fun and games? I'll take the fun out of it.

Even though it'll mean he gets full access to my body for the rest of the night because it was in the contract.

Even if he kills me. My mouth is writing checks my butt can't cash, but I'm too mad to think straight.

He paces forward, and I lock my legs so I don't cringe away. Now that he's close, I realize how much he towers over me. He could easily break me.

Why does that send a thrill through me? My mouth is dry, but my sex is wet.

He makes a show of checking his watch. "You have ten minutes until midnight."

Midnight. That will increase my payout tenfold.

He points to the woods, the opposite direction of the Lodge and any safety I might find.

"You run. I chase. Make it count."

This jerk. I hate him, even as my body responds to the fact that he's clothed and I'm naked and vulnerable to someone as big and powerful as he is.

He leans in, breaking my stunned spell. "Go."

Jaeger

She streaks away from me. Her beautiful bottom jiggles as she runs. She's all curves and delectable dimples, and my cock is tenting my pants. If I get any harder, it'll be torture to run.

I pick up my speed, embracing the pain. I let her get ahead so I can admire her nakedness whenever she streaks through a patch of moonlight.

"Five minutes," I call out. She dodges around a tree. I run left, making sure she sees me before turning right. I'm herding her deeper into the woods, where no one will hear her screams.

"One minute." There's a crash up ahead. I freeze and listen. She threw something to divert me, but she's sneaking through the bushes. I grab them and shake them, and she squeaks and hustles away.

"Ten. Nine." She's running again, weaving through the trees. "Eight. Seven."

She won't escape me.

"Five, four..." I increase my speed, running flat out until I draw even with her.

"Three." She's at my side, right in reach. She feints one way, but I anticipate her moves and follow her.

"Two." I'm right behind her, breathing down her neck.

"One."

I grab her and take us both to the ground. I wrap an arm around her and plant my free hand on the ground to break our fall. "Got you."

~

ELODIE

I SCREAM AND KICK OUT, but he's on top of me. He's holding his full weight off me, which means I have space to kick him. I writhe and get enough room to lash out, aiming for his crotch.

He jerks back, and I roll away. Freedom! I stagger to my feet and fly a few steps, only to trip over a rock. Something twinges deep in my ankle. I ignore it and limp three more steps before I get sacked again. This time, he lets me bear more weight. I thud to the ground, the wind knocked out of me.

Now he's got me. Now he's got me.

He's so heavy I feel crushed. I cry out, and he lifts off of me enough to let me breathe.

"Mmmm, good bunny."

"Get off!" I go crazy, striking out with elbows, feet, anything I can. I might as well be beating a wall. He's all hard muscle, and his scent covers me, a manly musk that actually smells good.

He seems content to lie here on top of me, pinning me to the ground with his weight. There's a club at my back, and I have the awful suspicion that it's his dick. He grinds it into me while burying his face in my hair.

Yep, that's his dick. And it's huge.

How the hell am I going to take that and survive?

He eases his full weight off of me, and his hands are everywhere, roaming. "You're so soft."

"Screw you."

"Mmm. I will." He finds my right breast and squeezes, plumping it in his hand. My arousal rises so fast that I gasp and claw at him to escape the pleasurable sensation.

He flips me over, takes both my wrists in one large hand, and pins them over my head. His lower half covers my legs so I can't kick. Now I'm naked and spread out, at his mercy. His eyes are the only thing I can see of his face, and they bore into me. The sight of the executioner's hood makes me panic all over again, but my body is still responding to his deft touches.

"Are you wet for me, bunny? Shall I check?"

I snarl but can't stop him. He slowly slides a hand down my front. He doesn't seem to mind the mess of leaves and mud. If anything, it excites him.

He reaches my pussy and hums. He's found my secret. I am soaking wet. He touches me with clever fingers, finding my clit and rubbing the right spot. He alternates a light touch with a rougher massage that makes me wild. The fact that he's restraining me only makes my core tighten more. After a minute, my orgasm is ready and roaring at the gates.

But I'm not going to make it easy on him.

I rise and try to bite the arm holding me down.

"Feral little thing." He thrusts two fingers into my mouth, and I clamp my teeth on them, but he just laughs. "Fight me all you want, little red." He pushes his digits further into my mouth, triggering the reflex at the back of my throat. I gag, saliva pouring into my mouth. "You're not going to win."

He pulls his fingers out, giving me a reprieve. But then he's stroking between my legs again, one thumb near my wet sex, the rest of his fingers delving between my ass cheeks.

"No," I yelp.

He chuckles darkly and smacks the side of my ass hard enough to make me still. "I own this now."

I freak out, flipping to my belly and making one last-ditch effort to crawl away. He drags me back and pins my arms apart. "We don't have to do this the easy way." He kicks my legs open and forces his knees between them. "I prefer it the hard way." His hood drapes over the back of my head. He's so big his body blankets mine. "And I'm beginning to think you prefer the hard way, too."

I try to buck him off and only succeed in rubbing my ass against his crotch.

He chuckles and releases my arms long enough to unzip himself. I struggle, but his weight has pinned me, and all too soon, he's setting his cock at my entrance. He rubs it there, and I freeze like a deer in the hunter's sight. He's going to take me now. No more preparation. No condom, no lube. He doesn't need the latter, and I agreed to the former. I have an IUD, and the club tests both of us to make sure we don't have STDs.

The head of his cock presses inside. I moan at the stretch. It hurts, and I want more.

His first thrust has me seeing stars. I'm cumming, clawing at whatever I can touch and thrashing underneath him. He growls and grips my arms, pinning me as he fucks me into the cold ground. I scrabble at the dirt, trying to find purchase. It's rough and primal, with the leaves in the trees hissing overhead and the moon a silent witness to our depravity.

His cock bottoms out, bumping my cervix, and I orgasm so hard light supernovas behind my eyes. It's been too long —years—since I've been with a partner. Years since I've been properly dicked down. And never like this. He hits all the secret, sensitive spots inside me. My womb quakes, and I'm drowning in wave after wave of bliss.

"Ah, yes." He sounds pained. My inner muscles are rolling, milking his cock. "Fuck yes, bunny. You have such a sweet"—thrust—"little"—thrust—"cunt."

Why am I so wet? Why does this thrill me? Why am I so

excited and closer to another orgasm faster than I've ever been?

It has to be the after-effect of adrenaline. In a study I read, people say they feel more attracted to someone when they meet during a stressful time. Like the adrenaline response, heightened heart rate, and sweaty palms come together in a perfect combination. Is it arousal? Or is it fear?

The body is easily confused.

My thoughts are gone, and my body is taking over. It probably thinks it's about to die; it's ready and going to ride every wave of pleasure before it goes. This is the survival response in its most amped-up, crazed form.

If I survive this night, I'll never forget being fucked by a monster in the deep woods. It'll be enshrined forever as the best fuck of my life.

Godsdammit.

Finally, the hunter grinds his hips against my ass and shudders. In a series of subtle jerks, his cock pumps cum into me, filling me up and setting off more deep flutters inside my belly.

He eases off me enough that I can push up to a sitting position on my left hip. Dirt is ground into my bare skin, and my hair is full of leaves and debris from the forest floor. I'm shivering and wincing from the bruises left by his rough handling. My sex is throbbing from his punishing thrusts, and so is my right ankle and not in a good way.

I try to rise, and my ankle twinges. It won't take my weight, but I'm desperate to get away. Without his warmth, I'm freezing, and cum is trickling down my leg. I crawl on my hands and knees until a shadow falls over me. His boots pace to my side, and he reaches down to dig his fingers into my messy curls. The tug sends pain shooting through my scalp as he draws my head back. "Going somewhere, bunny?"

I lash out, punching his knee and thighs, flailing in my attempt to hit his dick. He drags me to my knees and tries to lift me to my feet, but as soon as I put weight on my right ankle, I scream in pain and fall.

I end up back on my hands and knees, with him leaning over me. Something soft and warm falls over my head. Suffocating black fabric. He's taken off his hood and pulled it over my head. Blindfolding me.

Inside the hood, it's hot and smells like him. He's everywhere, his scent and touch my whole world. I thrash, but he's at my back, pinning me, finding my entrance, and pushing inside me again. I'm sore but sopping wet.

He subdues me, and my body gives in, lubricating to ease his way. The rougher he gets, the faster my orgasm rises. Grass and rocks tear into my naked flesh as he grinds me into the earth, and the bite of pain sends pleasure flaring through me. The harder he pounds into me, the harder I fight my own surging need. My orgasm is coming, inexorable. A nuclear explosion that will obliterate everything I am.

It's too much, but it's no use. The white-hot edge of pleasure slices into me, and I am undone.

I dig my fingers into the muddy earth and scream. Ecstasy crackles through me, breaking me apart. I can't escape. It surges again and again. I sob into the hood. The fabric is sodden, sticking to my face. It's stifling, but I'm grateful for a place to hide because I can't escape the pleasure pulsing through me.

"Yes, little red. You're so good, taking my cock like this. You feel so good," the Wolf keeps murmuring into my neck.

My mind is fragmented; I'm drifting in the dark. I pull his sweet nothings around me like a shelter.

"You take me so well." His cock swells, and he cums, spurting inside me over and over again. I lie there, taking it, and feel a faint sense of satisfaction. His cum is hot, and he's so deep he's battering my cervix. No man's ever filled me like this before.

He rises off me. Immediately, I miss his warmth, his weight. The sweat cools on my skin, and I shiver, coming back to myself. I'm bruised and chilled.

Before I can move, he pulls me up. I'm still in the dark, hot world of his hood. I can't see, so I'm reaching out to orient me, but he lifts me off my feet. The world tilts, and I cry out. I end up upside down, my hair and arms hanging down. He must have thrown me over his shoulder.

I tear off the hood and suck in fresh air, but it's all I can do. I'm in no position to do more than brace against his jean-clad ass and try to push myself up. He folds an arm over my legs and steadies me with a hand on my bare ass as he strides through the trees.

"What are you doing?" I cry. He smacks the back of my thigh.

"The night's far from over, little red. We're not done."

~

*J*AEGER

I PACE through the pines with the little redhead slung over my shoulder like a fresh kill. I'm heading southwest, following the trail only a select few know is here.

The Lodge isn't the only building on this land. There's a smaller outbuilding St. James and the Devil built in the woods. A second, smaller lodge. More of a cabin, if a place with all the luxury amenities of a five-star resort can be called a cabin.

I carry my prize through the woods. Once in a while, she starts to struggle, and I spank her ass to get her to behave. I like that she's still so amped up and ready to fight. She's hell-bent on getting away from me. I'd chase her all night and punish her for running with a hard fuck on the ground, until she understood the law of the hunt: what I catch, I keep. She's mine, all mine.

But she's shivering. And hurt. And I wasn't fully prepared for this, so I don't have my preferred toys on hand. Knowing St. James, he'll have the private cabin stocked with what I need.

I pick up my pace when I see the small building ahead. The lights blink on when I get close, and the redhead winces, hunching against me. For all her resistance, she was wet and ready for my cock. With every step, I breathe in the combined scent of her arousal and my cum—the sweetest perfume.

I key in the door code and step into the entryway's warm embrace. The heat's on. I was right. St. James made all the advance preparations.

The cabin is simple and laid out in modern lines. A touch of a button makes the gas fireplace flare with blue and orange flames before I cross the open living area and head for the sole bedroom. It's as big as the rest of the house, with an ensuite bathroom. The bathroom is my destination. The mirrors show a huge, half-naked brute covered in scars and tattoos, carrying a slight, leaf-covered bundle. We're both smeared with dirt, and her pale skin shows every mark and bruise from my brutal handling. Her ass is red where I spanked her.

She's going to be sore tomorrow.

I step right into the walk-in shower and set her down on a tiled bench. She blinks up at me, a dazed little bunny. Her hair is truly red and wild. Her makeup is smeared on her face, and a smattering of dark freckles show through.

She really is perfect.

"What is this place?" Her voice is hoarse.

"Somewhere we can be alone." I turn on the water. "Let's get you cleaned up." I check the temperature of the spray before I let it touch her skin, but she still flinches. Her hands and feet are freezing.

As much as I love to unleash the beast and have a good primal fuck, I also love the aftercare. I've always wanted a little pet to bathe and feed, stroke and keep.

And now I have one, and she needs my care.

There's a bottle of soap that pumps out expensive-smelling foam, so I fill my palm and use my hand to gently rub the dirt off her breasts. She was smart, rolling in the mud so she'd have some camouflage for her milky-white skin. It was a pleasure to roll with her in the dirt, and it's a pleasure now to clean her up.

"What are you doing?" Her words are slurred, exhaustion hitting after all that adrenaline.

"Getting you all clean." I don't add, *getting you ready for round two.*

I run my hand over her soft belly and thighs, washing away the dirt and leaves. Some of the dark marks won't wash away. I examine her bruises, and my cock swells in my jeans at the evidence of how I've claimed her.

Her sex is shaved bare, silky smooth. I let my touch linger there until her breath catches. She blinks and comes back to the moment enough to shove my hand away. I chuckle and let her deter me. For now.

Once I wash away the streaks of dirt from her feet, her ankle still looks a little pink. I make a mental note to check it in the morning.

"Tip your head back." I position her how I want her and rinse out her hair. I massage shampoo into her scalp and rinse it out carefully before working a rosemary-scented conditioner into the dark red strands.

The hair care products are specially made for curly hair. St. James really did think of everything.

While my bunny is relaxed and touch-drunk, I switch on the overhead spray and strip off my jeans. I clean myself quickly and turn to find her staring at me through the steam, her dark eyes wide.

"Enjoying the show?" I ask, facing her so she can get an unobstructed view of me soaping up my groin. My cock is granite hard and jutting toward her face.

Unconsciously, she licks her lips. I cup her chin and lean down to claim her mouth. I keep the kiss nice and easy, enjoying her soft sweetness. I slip my tongue in and explore her silky mouth. Her breath comes faster, and I fondle her left breast, thumbing her nipple until it's hard and erect. My dick is leaking by the time I break the kiss. "Ready for round two?"

~

ELODIE

.   .   .

THE HUNTER TOWERS OVER ME. He has dirty blond hair that hangs past his shoulders and stormy gray-blue eyes in dark rims. Soapy water runs down his back and abs, swirling over his ink. Every part of him is huge and powerful and hard as a rock. The sight of his dick makes my battered sex twinge. I can't believe I took him so easily.

And I can't believe I came so hard or so many times. I've only had a handful of partners, but it usually takes a vibrator and lots of coaxing to get my body to orgasm. He wrung climax after climax out of me like it was his due. And even though my body is aching in the aftermath, I want more.

I never thought getting chased and ravaged on the ground would be so thrilling. The hunter knew just how to manhandle my body and take control of my pleasure. He was rough in the woods in all the right ways. But now he's so careful, and the contrast is melting me. I might not know who he is, but my body is relaxing under his gentle touch.

I've never been so pampered, not even at the expensive spa I went to yesterday. The contract stipulated I get full body treatments, so I got waxed, plucked, tweezed, buffed, and polished until I was ready to scream. And it was all on St. James' dime.

Judging by the way the hunter can't stop stroking my bare pussy, this was all part of his fantasy. He also seems to enjoy taking care of me as much as I am enjoying being taken care of. I'm warm and sleepy, and when he leans down to kiss me, I'm too dazed to fight. I luxuriate under his lips, ready to twine my arms around his neck and pull him closer.

I wake up a little when he mentions round two. "What?"

He rubs a thumb over my lower lip, his eyes hooded as

he catalogs my responsiveness. His tattoos wind down his arms and hands, and he has a huge silver skull ring on his middle finger. "Did you think I was done with you?"

"It's over. You've won."

Is it my imagination, or did his dick just jump? "I did win. And now you're mine."

He doesn't give me a chance to run away or put weight on my leg. He wraps me in a big plush towel and gathers my hair into a smaller, microfiber one, bundling me up and carrying me out to the bed.

He lays me out naked, and the cooler air wakes me up further. He buckles thick, padded leather cuffs around my wrists, and that wakes me up even more. I make a sound of protest even as my pussy heats. I've never played with being tied down, but I've fantasized about it many, many times.

The fact that it's with a stranger is even more exciting.

"Shhh, bunny." He chains my arms above my head, somehow attaching them to the bed. "You don't need to fight anymore." He runs a hand down my bare chest, settling his palm on my plush belly. I can't deny he knows just how to touch me, awakening desires I didn't know I had. "Give in and let me lead."

He leans away, opening a drawer in a bedside table and pulling out a pink vibrator and a black bottle of lube. There's still an ache in my pussy from the way his cock battered me earlier, but my inner muscles flutter with anticipation. I yelp when he sets the vibrator against my sex and turns it on. "You're going to cum again for me. I want this sweet cunt nice and wet." He kneels between my legs so I can't close them. He's so massive. I don't know why I ever thought I could fight him and win.

A haziness drifts over me. I'm warm and comfortable

and at his mercy. The vibrator buzzes nonstop. My core tightens as my orgasm approaches while the rest of my muscles go lax with surrender.

The whole time, he studies me with his smoky blue eyes. He seems to know when I'm close to climaxing and clamps his hand around my neck. "Cum for me."

My orgasm burns through me with a bright, white heat. He keeps his fingers collaring me and leans down to kiss me again. This time, I raise my chin and drink him in, shuddering with the aftershocks of pleasure he's given me.

"Good bunny," he murmurs, and, in this moment, I don't hate his nickname for me.

He tosses the vibrator aside and lies down with his face between my legs. He rubs his stubbled cheek on my sensitive inner thighs. I shriek and tug on my chains, and he laughs. He switches to kissing the silvery stretch marks that streak my skin. His mouth inches closer to my pussy, and I whimper. I try to draw up my legs, and he clamps his huge hands on my thighs, holding them down. The move only makes me gush.

"Yes, bunny," he groans, his hips grinding into the bed. "Give me your sweetness." He dips his head and licks up my seam, making me arch off the bed. Only his cruel grip holding me open keeps me from levitating right off the bed.

He thrusts his tongue into my pussy, and I scream. His stubble scrapes my sensitive folds, adding a dimension to the pleasure. He finds my clit and laps at it until I'm writhing. He tears orgasm after orgasm out of me, then lifts my hips to spear me with his cock.

He sinks deep into me, fucking me like he wants to destroy my pussy. I fight the chains, and there's enough give for me to grab his shoulders and dig my nails into his inked skin. Marking him like he's marked me. The pain makes him roar and slam into me so hard we rock the bed.

I cum so hard I black out. From far away, I feel him pulsing in me, then freeing my wrists and dragging me into his arms. I sink into unconsciousness with his cock still inside me and him kissing my face and breasts and clinging to me like he'll never let go.

3

E *lodie*

BEFORE I EVEN OPEN MY eyes, I know it's late morning. Every inch of my body hurts to move as I peer into the gloom of the big bedroom. There's a heavy weight on my chest. A tattooed arm bulging with muscles.

The hunter lies on his stomach, his face planted in a pillow above my head. His hair has dried to a dark gold color, the coils draping down his back and obscuring a brutal-looking brand burned into the skin. It's a skull—the mark of Fraternitas. The design matches the big silver ring he's wearing on his left hand.

More proof that I'm in bed with a murderous monster.

I should count myself lucky I survived the night. But I'm not free of him yet.

I push his arm off and carefully slide out from under the

covers. He twitches, and I freeze, but he doesn't wake. I'm able to scoot to the edge of the bed.

The second my right foot hits the floor, I whimper and curl into a half-ball. My ankle is an angry red, swollen, and hot to the touch.

Dammit! How am I going to work my job with a hurt ankle? I can't afford the time off. A thousand dollars will barely cover the rent.

I might get ten thousand dollars, but I don't know if I made it to midnight. The jerk sleeping next to me might have lied just to toy with me.

First things first, though. My bladder is screaming at me.

I ease onto my left foot and hang onto the bed. It looks like it'll take ten steps to get to the bathroom. I try to limp, and pain knifes through me. I bite back a cry.

"Bunny," a deep voice mutters behind me. A strong arm wraps around my middle, and he pulls me against him.

His dick is hard. Again. Does it never rest?

"Let me go." I jab an elbow into his gut. His abs might as well be a brick wall. I probably hurt my elbow, and he doesn't seem to feel it.

"You're hurt." He runs a hand down my leg. I cringe when he touches below my knee and bite my lip to hold in my sob.

"I have to pee." I sound like a child holding back tears.

He lifts me easily and carries me to the bathroom. He sets me on the toilet, and I glare up at him. The pain has made me cranky and incinerated my survival instincts. "A little privacy?"

With a lazy smile, he saunters out of the bathroom but leaves the door open a crack. Somehow he knows when I finish because he's back, wearing his jeans this time. He picks me up, cradling me against his beautiful chest. I avert my eyes.

"Is my bunny shy?"

"No." I whip my head around and end up lost in his eyes. "And I'm not *your bunny*."

"No?" He lays me back on the bed and plants a palm on my chest so I can't move. "You have the cutest freckles." He brushes the tip of my nose.

I don't hate my freckles, but they are copious, so I usually cover them with an inch of concealer.

What's more unnerving is how he's touching me like he owns me. And my pussy likes it.

I push his hand away, watching him carefully to make sure I don't anger him. I'm fully aware of how he's clothed and I am not. He's only in a pair of jeans, but it would only take him a second to get undressed.

"The night's over. I'm no longer yours."

"Hmm." He doesn't say any more, just leaves the room, strutting as if he knows I'm studying the shifting muscles in his shoulders and back, and returns with a glass of water and two pills. "Painkillers. Take them."

I hesitate, but the pain wins the argument.

Did I make it to midnight? The question is on the tip of my tongue, but I don't want to engage with him any more than I have to.

He's typing on his phone. "I'm going to step out to make a call. Stay here and lie still."

I'm sitting up, intending to swing my legs over the side of the bed.

"Do it and I'll tie you down."

I stop moving and sink back against the covers.

He nods his approval and leaves.

The door opens, and then I hear voices, his voice

booming the loudest. I sit up and pull the blanket around me. I'm totally naked, and I don't like it, but I have no clothes, so I'll have to deal.

At least I'm clean, and my hair isn't the leaf-ridden mess I'd expected it to be. He washed it last night, and it dried with minimal frizz. A bad hair day is the least of my problems, but he gets points for taming my curls.

He returns with a tray of dishes covered with silver domes.

"What's that?" I ask.

He sets the tray down on the bed. It even has a little vase filled with white daisies and everything. "Breakfast." He lifts the biggest dome, revealing a plate of huge fluffy waffles covered in whipped cream and strawberry compote. "Catered from the kitchens at the Lodge." The delicious scent hits me, and my stomach growls so hard it can probably be heard from space.

He sits on the side of the bed, looking satisfied. "Eat. The doctor is on his way."

I pause with a cup of coffee halfway to my lips. "Doctor?"

"To examine your ankle."

I set down the cup with a click. "No."

His blue eyes narrow. "Bunny—"

"Don't call me that." I cross my arms over my chest.

He leans back, his mouth tipping into a half smile. He seems to find my recalcitrance amusing, which is annoying but better than making him mad. "What's your name?"

I press my lips together in a ridiculous show of defiance. I shouldn't feel reluctant to share my name with him after he's fucked me so thoroughly.

"Bunny..." he purrs in a way that tells me he'll make it my permanent name unless I give him what he wants.

"Elodie," I answer.

"Elodie." He savors my name like it's delicious. "I'm Jaeger." He pronounces it like the drink.

"Good for you," I say, making clear I am not pleased to meet him at all. "I've fulfilled the terms of the contract. And I made it until midnight, right?"

He nods.

Whew. That's some of the weight off my shoulders. Too bad all that cash has to go straight toward the debt hanging over my and my sister's heads.

"You have to let me go." I don't trust a flimsy piece of paper to shield me from a criminal, but it's all I've got. The gentle way he's cared for me hints at some secret code of honor.

"You're hurt. I can't in good conscience let you leave until the doctor's seen you."

How chivalrous. "I can't afford a doctor." I'm pissed that I have to admit that.

"It's no expense. Fraternitas takes care of its own."

I don't want to think too closely about that, so I turn my attention back to the coffee and waffles and bacon and sausage I find under another smaller silver dome. I might as well eat. I've earned it.

Jaeger watches me eat, a half smile on his handsome face. It's unnerving, sitting naked in front of such a perfect specimen of manliness. He watches me like a predator, following my every move. I do feel shy, which annoys me even more.

"Sorry, was some of this for you?" I pointedly take a piece of bacon and munch on it.

He leans in, slides a finger through the whipped cream, and holds my gaze as he licks it off slowly. Heat curls through my lower belly. I'm suddenly hungry for something else.

I shove the food away. I do not want to be attracted to this asshole. I still feel wrung out from all the orgasms he's given me. Not to mention the throbbing pain in my ankle.

He reaches in for more food, and the light catches his silver ring. The skull has empty eye sockets that give it a baleful stare.

"I should've known you're one of them."

He gives me a questioning grunt.

"Fraternitas." I point to the ring. "A thug."

He doesn't answer, only smiles in a way that makes my breath go faster. My insides curl, and there's a tugging sensation in my cunt in anticipation of him stroking me.

He leans down to kiss me. I surrender and sigh into his mouth, tasting the whipped cream.

Jaeger suddenly raises his head like a wolf catching a new scent. I expect him to say some crap about eating me for breakfast, but he crosses the room, pulls something out of a drawer, and drops it over my head. The fabric swallows me up, and I struggle until I realize he's putting a shirt on me. It's a man's black T-shirt big enough to fit him. It drapes over me like a dress.

It smells like him, leather and musk and a touch of something wild, like a midnight run through a pine forest.

The front door opens as Jaeger helps me tug the shirt down. "The doctor's here."

Great. I'm going to meet another member of the underworld. Some idiot who lost his medical license and scrapes out a living setting the bones of criminals.

But when the doctor walks into the bedroom, gorgeous with light brown skin and a shaved head, I sit up straight.

My heart pitter-patters and my body wakes up, realizing I'm surrounded by gorgeous men.

Then, I spy the skull ring on the doctor's middle finger. Crap, why am I so attracted to dangerous men?

"This is Elodie," Jaeger says.

The doctor nods to Jaeger before he turns to me. "Elodie, I'm Atticus. I'm here to examine you. Where does it hurt?"

I bite my lip as he handles my ankle with care. Jaeger lurks at my back, a heavy presence. Atticus touches something sensitive, and the flare of pain makes me reach for Jaeger. His hand catches mine, enveloping it in his warmth and strength. I squeeze as hard as I can, and he lets me.

"Looks like a grade two sprain," Atticus says.

"That sounds bad."

"It is. You must be in a lot of pain."

I shake my head and squeeze Jaeger's hand tighter. He touches my back with his free hand, stroking my hair. It's a light touch, ghosting over my curls, but it helps.

Atticus opens his case and pulls out a white pack. He crushes it until it turns cold. "Elevation and ice will bring the swelling down. I'm going to give you a compression wrap, but you're going to need to ice it every three hours."

"We'll set a timer," Jaeger says. I'm too worn out to protest the 'we.' The cold feels good on my heated skin.

Atticus opens a second section of his case, revealing row after row of baggies filled with pills. "And for the pain—"

"No drugs," I say quickly. "Nothing addictive."

Jaeger's fingers go still on my back, but then he keeps rubbing.

Atticus selects a bag of white pills. "You can get these over the counter."

"She's just had two aspirin," Jaeger tells him.

"These are better. Take three."

Jaeger takes the bag and tips three into my palm. Atticus continues to discuss my care with him right over my head.

"These can be combined with aspirin. She should ice it a little longer and use this to wrap it. Need a demo?"

"I've got it." Jaeger takes the wrap and more instant ice packs. "Ice every three hours, along with the pills."

"Rest, ice, compression, and elevation. Stick to a routine to get a jump start on the healing. I can check on her again in a few days."

I'm about to tell him that I can't afford his services when he says, "But she'll need to keep weight off the ankle for at least a few weeks."

"What?" I gasp loudly enough that the guys turn to me. "I can't do that."

"Bunny—"

"I have to work. I don't get sick leave. I can't take off weeks and weeks—"

"You have to heal," Atticus says. He looks sympathetic, but his tone is firm. "Rest is what you need."

I'm too dazed to argue. I've always been broke. I moved in with my sister Margot and her two kids after her ex left her. She's on disability in a subsidized apartment, but money's still tight. When I got my job as a waitress at Inferno, we both celebrated. I knew it was owned by the mob, but it paid well enough for me to look the other way. I deal with the temptation of drugs and alcohol and work as many shifts as they'll give me, but the pay isn't enough to touch my sister's medical bills, not to mention the debts that her ex skipped out on.

Last week, a thug showed up, demanding payment for a loan shark. Margot's ex borrowed from that loan shark, but he's in the wind, so we're the ones responsible. He threatened her and the kids. That's why I agreed to St. James' proposal and signed the contract so quickly.

The ten thousand has to go straight to that debt, but I still have to work to eat, to live. To pay my part of the rent so the creepy landlord doesn't throw my family onto the street.

Atticus packs up his case and shakes Jaeger's hand.

"Thank you, brother," Jaeger murmurs.

"Anytime. I'll see you soon, Elodie."

I shake my head. "I can't miss work."

Atticus sighs, and Jaeger claps his arm as if to signal, *I've got this.* The doctor exits, and Jaeger settles next to me. His arms come around me, and his lips press to my head.

It's not the comfort I'd choose, but it's comforting all the same. I lean into him, closing my eyes. If only this were a nightmare that would pass when I woke. Because last night feels like a dream, a hallucination. My ankle throbs like a heartbeat, reminding me this is real. The pills have dulled the pain, but it's still there.

Jaeger rubs my back, and his touch feels so good. How is it that this stranger's gentleness is the only thing holding me together? "It'll be okay, bunny," he says.

My eyes pop open. "No, it won't. I need that money from Inferno." I don't have an emergency fund or insurance or any of the things that an adult is supposed to have sorted out. "Why do you think I agreed to run around naked in the woods in the first place?" I turn my head. I hate sounding desperate. I hate that I am desperate.

He cups my chin with his big, tattooed hand and turns me to face him. "You'll be okay. We'll figure it out."

There's that 'we' again. "Sure," I agree because I'm too tired to do anything else. This situation is hopeless.

By midday, Jaeger will be long gone, and this will be a memory. If there's anything life has taught me, it's that men always leave. My father, my boyfriend, who lured me to the city and then abandoned me. Even my sister's ex, the father of her children. Men always leave.

Jaeger will be no exception. I'd bet what little money I have on it, plus the hundred thousand dollars I didn't win.

4

The city of New Rome is vast and dense, with millions of people calling it home. My sister Margot moved here as soon as she turned eighteen. A few years later, I followed a boy here and have been scrabbling to eke out a living ever since.

Jaeger insisted on driving me home. My neighborhood is poor but proud. His black and gold Lykan HyperSport does not fit in at all.

I had no idea being in a gang paid well enough to own such an expensive car. But Fraternitas is more than just a gang.

"You can drop me here," I say, pointing to the curb at the end of my block. The closer we get to the ancient apartment building where I live, the more my tension rises.

Jaeger ignores me. His car purrs right up to my door. The trio of men who always sit and smoke on a sidewalk bench straighten, their eyes wide.

"Let me out." I shoulder my purse and try the door, but it's locked.

He parks the car illegally and hops out, coming around

to my side. "I'll see you to your door," he says, like an old-fashioned suitor. He's supposed to be a Fraternitas thug. Who taught him manners?

"No—" I argue, but he's already unbuckled my seat belt and bundled me into his arms. Everyone on the sidewalk is staring like Jaeger's a celebrity. One of the smokers even scrambles up to open the door for him. Jaeger nods his thanks.

"This is ridiculous," I complain as he carries me in. The way my ankle is throbbing, I'm grateful I don't have to walk, but I'm not going to tell him that.

"No use fighting, bunny," he whispers in my ear. "You're hurt. You can't run."

I knew it. He's getting a kick out of this.

"Jokes on you," I mutter back. "The elevator's out. Has been for years." I point to the stairs. "I'm on the tenth floor."

He makes a *hmmm* noise but doesn't miss a step. Ten flights up the stuffy staircase usually leaves me sweaty and out of breath. Jaeger isn't even breathing hard. I start to struggle as soon as he reaches my floor.

"Put me down." I don't want my sister and niece and nephew to see me like this. It's bad enough that I have a wrapped ankle, and I'm wearing brand new clothes—a sky-blue lounge set and cream-colored lingerie miraculously appeared after Atticus left, along with my purse.

He sets me down and steadies me until I'm stable, holding the wall.

"You need to leave." If I sound ungrateful, I am. It's his fault I'm hurt.

I want him gone, no matter how much I know I'll fantasize about our night together. Sometimes we get what we want, but what we want isn't always good for us. Asshole men are my cocaine. I've been addicted before; I'm not getting sucked in again.

"You need help."

No argument there. "I know. I just don't want yours." There, I've made myself clear. Too bad I can't look directly into his stunning blue eyes as I say it.

"All right, bunny. I'll go."

I sag against the wall. Thank the gods. It's a good thing he agrees because I have no way of forcing him to do anything. I'll just ignore the way my body cries out for his. How I'm already missing his warmth and scent. There's no reason for me to want him around.

Because I learned a long time ago that cravings aren't logical.

"Here." He pulls out a battered, brown leather wallet and extracts a wad of bills, all hundreds.

I tense at the sight of that amount of money. "St. James said the money will be in my account." Paid through Inferno, marked as a bonus.

He doesn't urge me to take it. He just tucks it right in the pocket of my joggers, holding my gaze.

A flush rolls over my cheeks and chest. I'm not ashamed of sex work, but standing so close to his burly form, it's impossible to forget how I earned this cash. How savagely he broke my body in.

How hot we were together.

His eyes burn. I swallow. I don't want to take this money. I don't want to need it.

But I do.

"Bye," I whisper because that's all that's left. There's so much unspoken between us that will never be said. That's just the way it is. The way it has to be.

I watch him pace to the stairs. He pauses, the muscles in his back working like he's wrestling with himself.

A rush of desire hits me so hard that I get dizzy. *Turn around. Don't leave.*

It's the craziest thing I've ever felt and all the more potent because it's true and as real as the gravity holding my feet to the floor.

But he does leave. I wait until his bright head disappears before rapping on the door.

The second my sister opens it, I know something's terribly wrong. My sister doesn't look like she's slept all night. Her eyes are puffy like she's been crying, and her toddlers, Tyson and Janie, are shrieking in the background.

"Where have you been?" she hisses, looking left and right as if expecting someone to leap out at us. "I've been calling you."

"My phone died." I push past her, propping myself up on the wall, limping as quickly as I can to the couch. "I had a job."

The apartment's a mess. Toys in every color cover the floor, the TV plays a kid's cartoon on low volume, and the place smells like dirty diapers and spilled juice with a faint undertone of mold. In the grimy window, an ancient AC unit cranks out warm air. It leaks water so long there's a black trail from the window to the floor.

This place is home. But instead of the relief and comfort I get from the depressing but familiar surroundings, I have a brief flash of longing for the resort-level cabin where I spent the night.

I sink into the crumb-covered couch. Margot runs to get Tyson out of his high chair. He and his older sister have perpetual bedhead and run around in sagging diapers, but they seem happy. I have to believe my niece and nephew know they're loved and that we've done our best to protect them from the crushing stress of bills, deadbeat dads, and crappy apartments. I can only hope.

Margot gets the kids set up in front of the TV and returns to me.

My older sister was always beautiful. She dropped out of high school and headed to the big city to start her modeling career. She ended up pregnant with Janie instead.

Her multiple sclerosis diagnosis came soon after Tyson, which was when her baby daddy left.

She needs expensive medication. The disease attacks her nervous system, and if she deteriorates, we're afraid social services will take away her kids.

I pull the money from my joggers and hand it to her.

She sucks in a breath as if I've handed her a snake. "What is this?"

"Payment. There's more where that came from. We can pay off Trey's debt."

Instead of looking relieved, her face crumples, and she sags to the couch.

"What is it? What's wrong?"

"It's too late. He came back." She's whispering, glancing nervously at her kids and away.

"Baldie?"

She nods. The first time the loan shark's thug came around, we called him Baldie and laughed behind his back. He was looking for Trey. The next time, he'd told us Trey was gone and that his debt had fallen to us. If we didn't pay, he would break our legs. We gave him our rent money as a stop gap and quit making Baldie jokes.

"When?"

"Last night. Pounded on the door so hard, I thought he'd wake the kids." She runs a hand through her hair. It's a gorgeous auburn that usually falls in a silky wave. But right now, it's dank and flat, like she's been running her sweaty hands though it nonstop. "He said now we owe double."

"Double? How can that be?" Trey had been stupid enough to run up a gambling debt with a loan shark named "Umberto the Executioner." Skipping town was the smartest thing he's ever done.

Too bad he left a destitute family behind.

Margot shrugs. "Interest. They can do what they want, and there's nothing we can do about it."

The full horror descends. The ten thousand I've earned won't touch the new amount. Not even close. And I have no idea how to earn more.

"He's coming back," Margot says. "He said he'll take the kids until we pay him."

Over my dead body. "That's not going to happen."

"I don't know what to do." She's clutching the collar of her shirt and pulling it up like she wants to disappear. Like a child pulling a blanket over her head because if she can't see the monster, it isn't real.

"Here's what we're going to do." I have a new plan. It's not great, but it's something. "You're going to pack what you can for you and the kids. Not everything, just what you need. And I'm going to drive you to the train station. He can't take the kids if he can't find them."

"Where am I going to go?"

"West Virginia. Aunt Carol. Remember her?"

Margot straightens, a little color returning to her cheeks. "Mom's half-sister? Is she still alive?"

"She is. I send her a card every New Year." The summer I spent with her, weeding the garden and learning to can green beans and tomatoes, was the best season of my life. "She'll be surprised but glad to see you. And she loves kids."

Best of all, she owns a trailer and a remote patch of land on a mountain. The loan shark won't be able to find Margot there.

"Get your suitcase," I say, and Margot jumps up as if she were waiting for the command. She hasn't thought to ask me what I'll do while she's on the run. Which is fine because I don't know. I could go with her and the kids, but it might attract too much attention and slow them down. Better that someone stays here and keeps the lights on, a decoy to draw the predators in.

I just have to figure out what to do when the thugs come for me. It's not like I'll be able to run.

I sag back on the couch. The pain meds are wearing off, and my ankle is throbbing again. I need to ice it.

A hurt ankle is the least of my worries.

For a blissful second, I recall last night and running through the forest. The cool air on my skin and nothing but the threat of the hunter behind me.

Everything in life comes down to a simple calculation of survival. You escape; you live. You get caught, and it's lights out.

Except for last night, when it was just a game. Running was a thrill, and capture meant orgasms. I never thought I'd enjoy surrendering. Jaeger had made sure I did.

But he's gone now, and all I have left are my real-life problems.

Margot's piling up bags outside her bedroom door.

"Don't forget your medication," I remind her. I hope she has enough. Just another thing added to the list of things to worry about.

For a crazy moment, I wish Jaeger were here. It makes no sense, but I imagine standing in his arms, leaning on his strength. *It's going to be okay, bunny. We'll figure it out.* It's a stupid fantasy because a man like Jaeger means more problems. But it's never going to happen, so it's safe to dream of his beautiful face and perfect, woodsy scent.

Then I open my eyes, and reality punches me in the face.

My ankle is pulsing with pain. I peel back the wrap a little and wince at how puffy it looks. My sprain might be the least of my problems, but I can do something about it.

I'm about to brave the walk across a block-covered floor to the kitchen for some ice when there's a creak from the hall outside the apartment. My heart trips.

Someone pounds on our front door.

Margot appears at the bedroom door, wide-eyed and trembling.

"Go hide," I whisper, getting off the couch. She doesn't argue and runs to get the kids, pulling them away from their toys. She tells them a story about playing hide and seek as she bundles them into the bedroom. I wait until the bedroom door closes before limping to check the peephole.

A square chin covered in blond stubble greets me. Jaeger's back. I'm frozen, unable to believe it.

"Let me in," says the Big, Bad Wolf.

What the heck?

I rip open the door and lean on it, trembling.

"I brought donuts," he says as if this will explain his presence. He holds up a pink rectangular box tied with string.

"Why?"

He's already pushing his way in. "You shouldn't be on your feet." He takes my arm and lends his weight, helping me to the couch.

"You're the one who knocked." My peeved voice comes out breathless. I sink onto the couch with relief.

He pulls out a pack of instant-ice and fusses over my leg.

"Did you take your meds?" He lopes to the kitchen and comes back with a glass of water before I can answer.

"Elodie?" My sister peeks out of the bedroom and tenses at the sight of the huge, tattooed enforcer leaning over me with a glass of water.

"It's okay." I wave her over. "He's not here to hurt us."

As if to prove my point, Jaeger pulls the bottle of pain pills out of my purse and shakes a few out onto my palm.

"This is my..." I start and realize that the only way I can finish the sentence is *my one-night stand, who paid to fuck me after he chased me through the woods.* "Jaeger. Um. He brought donuts."

My sister just stares. For a moment, I see Jaeger through her eyes: a six-foot-tall stack of sexy blond. She's used to skinny male model types. Jaeger could probably bench-press ten of them.

"Nice to meet you," Jaeger rumbles, and he sounds so civilized my eyes almost pop out of my head. "Would you like a donut?"

Margot swallows as if she's unsure if this is a trap. The only reason big, burly men have shown up to our door is to shake us down.

The kids have no such qualms.

"Donuts," Janie screeches, squeezing past her mother. Her two-year-old brother takes up the chant in his toddler-speak, "Do-nuh, do-nuh."

Jaeger flips the box open.

"Uh, Margot, why don't you take these?" I grab the box and hand it to her before the kids get their grubby hands on it. "You can cut them into pieces for the kids? I need to talk to Jaeger a sec."

Still pale, Margot's eyes dart to Jaeger's skull ring and

away. She presses her lips together and leads the screaming children to the kitchen.

I stare up at Jaeger. "What are you doing here?" I whisper. "I thought you were going to go."

"I did go. I got donuts." He looks around, taking in the shabby apartment—the frayed carpet and water stains on the ceiling. Meanwhile, I'm drinking him in. He looks unreal, his hair shining golden in the dim light. Like he's full color, and the rest of the world is faded.

I try to convince myself his presence is a complication I don't need, but my body's quivering like he's the best thing I've ever seen.

"This is where you live? With your sister?"

I stiffen. He doesn't have the right to ask questions. I don't ask him how he knows Margot is my sister.

"Uh, she's leaving."

He nods, glancing at the suitcase and bags piled outside the bedroom. "When?"

"Right now, actually. Margot," I call to her. "You should get the kids ready. I'll call a cab." I'll have to use my almost maxed credit card to pay for it. As soon as the ten thousand I've earned hits my account, I'll use some of it to get out of here and find a way to get the rest to Margot and my aunt.

I pull out my phone, but it's dead.

"I'll do it," Jaeger announces. "And let me help you with the bags."

"No," I protest. I struggle to my feet, but he takes my shoulder and gently pushes me back down. I crumple under his stormy stare. I can't fight him, and I don't know why I would when it hurts to stand.

"What's wrong with her ankle?" Margot has less of a deer-in-the-headlights look now. She brushes her hair behind her ear, blinking up at Jaeger. She's not flirting; she's just using her looks to her advantage. It usually works—even tired with limp hair and dark circles under her eyes, she's cat-walk-model stunning.

But Jaeger doesn't seem to notice.

"She hurt it last night," Jaeger answers for me. I don't know why they're talking over my head when I'm right here.

My sister's stare sharpens. "You were with her last night?"

"We don't have time for this," I interrupt. I don't want her to know the details of how I earned the cash, and we don't have time. The thugs could be here any minute. "You have to get the kids out."

"Right." Margot hustles, getting the kid's sticky faces and hands cleaned up and bundling them into clothes. Jaeger picks up her suitcase and the few extra bags she's managed to pack. Janie gets her own tiny backpack. Tyson sucks on the matted fur of his favorite teddy.

I fight tears, holding open my arms to give them kisses and a final farewell.

I recite my Aunt Carol's address until Margot memorizes it. "Don't write it down," I tell her. "And don't call me. They might be able to track it." From the corner of my eye, I sense Jaeger's attention focused on me. So far, he's been quiet and gone with the flow, but any second, he might speak up and start asking questions. And I don't know what he'll do next.

He's a wild card in this mess. I don't like it. I want to know why he came back, but again, I have a whole list of problems, and his appearance doesn't even crack the top ten.

"Don't use your cards, either. Pay cash for everything so you don't leave a trail. I'll send you more cash as soon as I can," I promise.

Margot nods and leans down to give me a hug. It's

surprising because she's not usually the hugging type. It makes more sense when she whispers in my ear, "Are you sure you're okay?" I'm sure she's wondering why a huge, tattooed Fraternitas thug is bringing me donuts.

"Positive." I plaster a big ole fake smile on my face and push her away. "Think of this as a vacation."

She stands, still looking unconvinced.

"Go," I urge with everything in me.

Her mouth snaps shut, and she steers the kids away. "Come on, everybody. We're going on an adventure." Her voice is cheery and bright in a way that tells me she's a second away from snapping.

I scoot to the edge of the couch, wanting to go walk her to the stairs, but Jaeger places a hand on my shoulder again. "Stay."

Heat flushes my face. It's anger, I tell myself. Not a reaction to his touch. "I'm not a dog," I snap.

He quirks a blond brow and touches his thumb to my lips. Just like that, my body melts into a puddle. My body quivers. My breasts swell. I'm ready for him to take me right here, right now.

Worse, he knows it.

"Stay," he repeats and heads out behind my sister. He leaves the door open.

I guess he's planning on coming back. I fall back on the couch and rub my face. Things are happening too quickly, but at least I won't worry about the kids. I couldn't live with myself if anything happened to them.

They'll all be safe. They have to be. Now, I just have to figure out how to survive.

On top of that, I have to find out what Jaeger is doing here. Why can't life be simple?

Men always leave. Except, apparently, Jaeger.

He came back.

The steps outside the door creak. "Did everything go okay?" I ask without opening my eyes.

"It most certainly did not," a peevish voice answers.

My eyes fly open. Mr. Wilson, our creepy landlord, stands over me. His BO hits me as he leans down, scowling. "Is your sister going on a trip? You both owe me back rent."

Great. Here's another one of my problems, now moved to the top of the list. "I'll get it to you," I lie. I'm a sitting duck in this apartment. As soon as I can, I'm going to run. Get to an ATM and get out as much cash as I can. I'll find a by-the-week hotel room, pay with cash, and lie low.

I've spent my life running from my problems, so why stop now?

"You said that last week." He steps closer, and his stench wafts over with me, making me gag. "There've been a lotta men lurking around here. Asking 'bout you both. They don't seem very nice. I try to protect my renters—" He's lying. He'd sell out his grandmother to save his own skin. "But they look dangerous. I'll have to tell them everything I know unless you make it worth my while."

I'm too tense to breathe. As threats go, this is a good one. He could spill everything to the loan shark's thugs, and they could intercept Margot and the kids before she has time to get out of the city.

Godsdamn this man. He's a loser who preys on people weaker than him. When there's blood in the water, even the bottom feeders swarm to get their pound of flesh.

"I don't have any cash on me." I raise my empty hands.

He shrugs. "We could figure something out." He's close enough that I can see the old stains on his faded black pants. "Your sister is the pretty one," he says with a leer. "But you work at that mob club, right? I bet you suck dick real good." His hands go to his zipper, and I cringe back, averting my head to avoid smelling his stench and seeing the contents of his pants.

A shadow falls over us both. "Get away from her," Jaeger rumbles softly. Mr. Wilson doesn't have time to look up from his half-opened pants before Jaeger grabs his shirt and sends him flying across the room.

I clap my hands over my mouth. I didn't even hear Jaeger come up the stairs. He's stealthier than a man of his size has any right to be. I'll have to remember that.

Mr. Wilson staggers to his feet. His pants are now at his ankles, and I try not to look too closely. At least he's wearing boxers.

"Who are you?" He gapes at Jaeger.

"You don't want to know." Jaeger clamps a hand on the back of his neck and sends him careening toward the door. "You're no longer welcome here."

Mr. Wilson is stupider than I thought because he hits the door jamb and stands his ground. "It's my building. I have rights! She owes me rent."

Faster than I can follow, Jaeger shoots forward. The next thing I know, Mr. Wilson is falling into the hall, his mouth full of bills.

"There." Jaeger kicks at a fallen wad of cash. "That should cover it. And spread the word: Elodie and her family are under my protection."

Mr. Wilson sputters, spraying cash, and Jaeger shuts the door in his face.

I still have my hands over my mouth, panting like I've run up ten flights of stairs. I know Jaeger is violent, but watching it unfold before my eyes is another story.

And now I'm alone with him. What is happening? Why is he here?

Why am I under his protection?

Slowly, Jaeger swivels to face me. His face is blank and scary. I know he won't hurt me, but he's intimidating as hell right now. He moves closer, blocking the weak light streaming through the window, and his shadow swallows me whole.

"Now, bunny," he says in a soft voice that sends chills up and down my arms. "You're going to explain to me what's going on."

5

J aeger

SHE STARES UP AT ME, her freckled face so young in the morning light. It's all I can do not to drop to the couch and pull her in my arms to assure her that everything will be okay. But I'm still filled with rage after dealing with the sleazy landlord. I don't dare touch her in case the beast breaks free. I've spent my life on edge, ready to fight, and she's a tiny, fragile creature. I won't risk hurting her.

"I can explain." She hesitates. "Did Margot get a cab?" Even helpless and in pain, she's so focused on helping others.

This is why my bunny needs me. I knew I shouldn't leave her alone. The world is cold and cruel and gobbles up tiny bunnies for breakfast.

She needs a Big, Bad Wolf at her side. I got here in the nick of time.

"I did one better," I tell her. "I called her a private escort. They'll get her out of the city and put her in a hotel for the night." By then, my network of contacts will have forged new identities for Margot and her young children. Elodie's sister will get new papers, a burner phone, and an escort all the way to her final destination.

Whatever Elodie's situation is, she doesn't have the experience to handle it. I've spent my life dealing with sticky situations. Mostly, I murder people to solve them, so this is a nice, relaxing change of pace.

And helping children has always been a priority. If I had my way, no one who touches a hair on a child's head would live.

No one touches my bunny, either.

"Your sister will be safe. I'll make sure of it."

She blinks at me, her forehead furrowed as if she doesn't believe me. "Why?" she finally says.

"Because you're now under my protection."

"But...why?"

I stare down at her. I don't answer because I don't know how to put my urges into words. "Why didn't you tell me you were in trouble?"

She snorts. "Why would I? I don't usually explain my life story to my one-night stands."

I grit my teeth against the sting of jealousy. My voice deepens to a growl. "Do you have many of them? One-night stands?"

She shakes her head. "It's none of your business. But no."

I relax. It doesn't matter who she's been with, I remind myself. It only matters that from here on out, she's with me.

"But they don't usually stick around," she says. Her tone is accusing, as if she's challenging me to leave.

Too bad. I'm not going anywhere. Not without her.

I caught my perfect prey, and I want to keep her.

I cup her face in my tattooed palm. Her eyelashes flutter. Poor bunny. She's hurt and needs rest to heal.

"I'm taking you away from here."

She jerks out of my hand and glares at me. "If you're here for more of what you got last night, you're going to be disappointed." She waves a hand at her ankle. "Like you said, I can't run away."

Sweet rabbit. Doesn't she know I'm enjoying this new game? Caring for her is just as fun as the chase. I never thought I'd enjoy keeping what I've caught, but with her, I do. It satisfies the beast.

"Tell me why you wanted Margot and the kids to leave."

She sighs. "Her ex borrowed from a loan shark and couldn't pay, so he split. The loan shark's been sending his thugs to threaten us. We've been holding him off by giving him our rent money." She picks at the fraying couch cushion. "Why do you think I took a sex work gig that involved me running naked through the woods? For my health?"

Grumpy bunny. I love it when she snaps at me.

"How much do you owe?"

"It was thirteen thousand. Now, apparently, it's doubled." She rubs her forehead. "I guess that's how loan shark interest works."

"What is this person's name?"

"Umberto the Executioner."

I've heard of him. He operates outside the city, across the river, so as not to infringe on Fraternitas' territory and incur our wrath.

"So far, they've been fine with the rent money," she says. "But I guess last night, one of them threatened to take the kids."

"He will not touch a hair on their heads." Or yours, I add silently.

She looks so defeated, slumped on the couch with her foot propped up.

I squat down so we're at eye level and cup the back of her neck. I squeeze lightly, giving her a slow, gentle massage. "I'll fix it."

Her gaze darts to me and away. But she leans into my touch. She knows she needs my help, even though she's fighting her desire for me.

I can work with that. "You're not staying here."

"What?"

I gather her things into her purse and lift her in my arms. "You're coming with me."

"Jaeger, no." She pushes at my shoulder, but it might as well be a swipe of a kitten's paw.

I smile at her. I like it when she tries to fight me. It's adorable.

I hoist her closer, and she meets my gaze. She flushes and looks away.

Interesting.

I don't have time to study her responses to me—the red creeping up her freckled cheeks, the catch in her breath, the way she leans into me even though she's protesting. I carry her out of the apartment and make it down one flight of stairs, only to be met by two bald goons on the stairwell. They're clearly heading to Elodie's apartment. One of them has a bat propped on his shoulder and is whistling as he climbs.

Elodie grabs my shirt, gripping it tightly.

"It's okay, bunny." I'm going to have to put her down to deal with these men. Leaving her unguarded is not my preference, so I'll have to make the fight quick.

She's not listening. "It's them." Her face blanches. "That's the guy Umberto sent. I don't have the money to pay them yet."

She's not giving them a dime. "You won't need it," I tell her. "You have me."

She stares at me, unseeing. I have no choice but to set her on a dirty step. "Stay here. I'm going to deal with this."

No one threatens my bunny and lives.

ELODIE

JAEGER LEAVES me leaning against the railing and turns to face the thugs. The first one is Baldie, the ass who's been shaking us down. The second is a carbon copy of him and holding a bat. He doesn't look like a guy who likes to play baseball, which means the bat is used to hit other things.

Baldie stops on the landing below as Jaeger blocks his passage up the stairs. "We don't want no trouble. We got business with her." He points to me.

"Wrong," Jaeger says. "If your business is with her, it's with me."

Baldie and his buddy share a glance. "So be it." The second guy swings the bat back, ready to strike.

Before Baldie can move, Jaeger leaps and lands on him. At least, I think that's what happened. It's hard to follow his movements. A big guy shouldn't be able to move so fast.

Baldie goes down with Jaeger on top of him. There's shouting and a crack, and Jaeger's rising from a limp body. Baldie's head lies at an impossible angle, his eyes staring at nothing.

The second thug is already scrambling up the stairs, headed toward me. The weaker prey. I scoot back on the dirty tile as fast as I can, biting back a cry of pain. It hurts so bad that I can't get away.

Turns out I don't have to. Halfway up the stairs, the second thug falls on his face. Jaeger drags him back and kicks him over. "You fucked with the wrong woman." suddenly, Jaeger has the bat. I cover my eyes.

"No, no, please—" There's a thwack, then nothing but screams. I wish I could cover my ears.

But I peek through my fingers to watch the blood spatter. The savage part of me is hungry for the sight and scent of the blood of my enemies.

Jaeger tips what's left of the man over the railing of the stairs. The bloodthirsty part of me crows with delight, pleased at how he's solved my problems with brutal efficiency.

Jaeger whips around, looking for me. Flecks of red cover his perfect face and his shining hair. When he sees that I'm okay, a cruel smile curves his lips.

He stalks my way, taking the stairs three at a time. I don't know whether to cringe away or cheer. I settle for holding still as he scoops me up and cradles me against his chest. He carries me the rest of the way down the stairs, carefully stepping over Baldie's body.

Cries in the stairwell echo above us as people open their doors to find the blood and bodies. We pass thug number two on our way out the door. I avert my eyes from the body.

The sun blazes on our faces the second we walk outside. Jaeger doesn't hesitate. His car is again illegally parked in front of the building, but no one has touched it.

He sets me gently in the passenger seat and buckles me

in. I let him. I'm not catatonic, but I'm taking in everything around me like it's a movie playing on a screen.

He pauses, and I blink up at him. I don't know if I'll ever stop reliving the moment he took a bat to the thug who threatened me in one breath and screamed for mercy the next.

Jaeger cups my cheek, and I startle, coming back to the present. He looks like a Viking, returned from pillaging new lands. But his touch is gentle.

He doesn't speak. He swipes my cheek with a thumb and then pulls away to shut my door.

I watch him slip some cash to the old men who sit on the bench. They smile up at him, calling him 'sir.' One of them salutes him.

Jaeger gets into the driver's side. "*Vini vidi vici*," he murmurs with that cruel smile. At least, I think that's what he says. How does a guy like him know Latin?

The Lykan engine roars to life. The car goes zero to sixty, and just like that, my apartment building is in the rear view mirror and disappearing.

I don't know where he's taking me.

I can only hang on for the ride.

JAEGER

MY BUNNY LIES in my king-sized bed, tucked on her side with her ankle carefully elevated. She passed out almost as soon as I set her down. The events of last night and today wiped her out.

Good. She needs rest to heal.

I can't stop looking at her. Her hair is a dark flame against the blue blankets. Her eyes are closed, and her breath comes softly, but every once in a while, her nose twitches, and she mumbles something. Her forehead knots until I reach down and lay my palm on her knee. My touch settles her every time.

She's beautiful like this, asleep and serene. I like her like this, but I also like her when she's glaring up at me, eyes snapping. She has dark eyes unlike any I've ever seen. They're almost purple with a reddish tint, like mulberries. And her freckles are a wonder. I want to trace each one, even though my rough, tattooed hands on her pure, freckled skin look obscene. Like a demon's claws on an angel's wings.

She was frightened today on the stairs, but she didn't shrink away from me. For a moment when she looked at me, there was a savage excitement in her dark eyes. She didn't just accept my violence; she embraced it.

She was made for me.

The money Fraternitas makes affords me this luxury penthouse, but I've never felt it was home. Not until now. Before Elodie, I only came here to crash between completing my duties for Fraternitas. The brotherhood is all that matters.

Now, I'm getting a glimpse that life might have more to offer. It's like I've been living in darkness and someone flipped on the lights.

There's not a lot of space in my life for soft, sweet things. The world is violent and cruel, and I've made myself even more violent and cruel to survive it. But maybe surviving isn't all there is. Maybe after all the struggle, there can be a reward. The wolf can make space for a sleepy little bunny in his den.

Maybe this one I get to keep.

6

E *lodie*

ONCE AGAIN, I wake up in a strange but beautiful space. Jaeger's bedroom is dim and contains nothing but the gigantic bed I'm lying in and two matching bedside tables with lamps. No other furniture. But the sheets and blankets are soft and smell like him.

There are worse places to wake up. I try to sort through everything that happened—the night in the woods, my return to the apartment, Margot leaving with the kids—and my brain stutters when it gets to Jaeger's body count.

I've never seen a murder before. Much less two. It makes the violence he committed against Mr. Wilson seem friendly by comparison. And at that moment, that violence had been the worst I'd ever seen.

I have to be careful. I'm in the wolf's lair with no way to

escape. At least until my ankle is feeling a little better. The last thing I remember is Jaeger carrying me into his penthouse. The place was dark but I got a sense of how vast it is, and how empty. It's like this bedroom, furnished in a modern style but with no personal touches. He might as well be living in a hotel.

There's a glass of water on the bedside table next to my pain meds. Two pills are sitting in the open cap. I take them and scoot to the edge of the bed so I can go to the bathroom.

Once again, Jaeger appears without a sound to alert me that he's close. How does he always appear when I most need him?

"Sleep well?" he asks. He looks wide awake and alert, the bastard.

My bladder is screaming, and I'm not fully awake, so I just grunt and hold up my arms.

He comes and picks me up, carrying me to a gorgeous bathroom with black and gray marble floor and walls, a sleek white tub, and a cavernous shower area. He leaves me on the toilet in the private alcove, and through the door, I hear the sound of water turning on.

He returns to help me hobble to the bath. I bite back a squeal of delight when I see the tub filling with bubbles. I don't stop to ask why a mafia thug has a brown-sugar-scented bubble bath in his luxury bathroom. It either came with all the expensive, modern furnishings, or he bought it for me. The thought that he ordered things for me makes my belly quiver, and I don't want to dwell on that too long.

He lets me lean on him so I can strip off the cami top and underwear I wore to bed, and I sink into the warm water with a groan. He sits on a stool beside me, watching me with that satisfied curve to his lips.

I don't even care that I'm naked and he's fully clothed. Most of the time we've spent together, we've been in various states of undress.

It's a bit weird when he produces a washcloth and, instead of handing it to me, proceeds to wash me himself.

My cheeks heat from the hot bath water and also the way he takes his time rubbing the washcloth over my skin. I remember how he washed me in the shower after our primal play. He seems to love the aftercare, but it's so intimate that I find it hard to meet his bright blue gaze. I fight the urge to shy away.

The washcloth swirls lower and lower, washing my belly on its way down between my legs.

"I can do it," I gasp and catch his wrist. But he doesn't relinquish the washcloth, and I'm not strong enough to wrestle it out of his hands. He holds my gaze with that smirk on his handsome face and rubs the cloth between my legs. I shudder under his perfect touch.

All too soon, he's pulled the washcloth away. I slip deeper into the water as he washes down my legs and examines my swollen ankle.

"Atticus is coming by to examine you again," Jaeger says.

It's only been a day since the doctor saw me. I haven't even had a basic checkup for years, and now I'm getting multiple doctor visits within twenty-four hours.

But Jaeger's in charge, so I say nothing.

"I have something to show you." He pulls out his phone and holds it up so I can see the screen.

It's a picture of Janie smiling in a sunny yard, Tyson bent over and playing in the grass behind her. They're both surrounded by tall plants staked with colorful sticks. Tomato plants, I realize, and then I understand what I'm looking at. This is Aunt Carol's backyard and garden. The picture is from this morning.

"They made it." My voice comes out choked up. *They're okay.*

"My men decided it would be safer for them to drive through the night. Your aunt was surprised to see them, but she welcomed them immediately, and they've settled right in."

I study the picture, drinking in the kids' smiles. They look right at home.

"They'll have new identities soon as well," Jaeger says. "No one will be able to find them."

My worry rears its head. "Margot has MS. She needs meds, insurance. If she can't—"

"Hey." Jaeger sets his hand on my knee. Under his touch, the anxious flutters calm. "It'll be okay. We'll make sure she's set up with a doctor. In the meantime, Atticus can prescribe what she needs from here."

Another benefit of having a mafia doctor on call.

The rush of relief leaves me dizzy. My biggest problem was solved, just like that.

"Thank you," I say. Without thinking, I reach up and cup the back of his neck, pulling him close so I can press my lips against his. I'm dripping soapy water on the back of his shirt, but he doesn't seem to mind. He slants his head and takes control, plunging his tongue into my mouth. My nipples harden, and by the time he breaks the kiss, I'm panting.

He brushes bubbles off my chest. "Bunny," he murmurs and slides his hand lower. This time, I don't stop him. I lean back and open my legs, accepting his skilled touch on my folds. He knows just how to press, to rub, but in the end, it's the intense gleam in his eyes that sends me over the edge.

And then, his hand is gone, and he's standing up to strip

off his T-shirt and jeans. I'm dazed, my insides still quivering, when he lifts me out. Water and foam flood over the beautiful tile and plushy bath mats, but he doesn't seem to notice. He sets me on the marble vanity and moves closer to position his cock at my entrance, ignoring my protests.

"Jaeger, no. I can't, my ankle—"

"Shhh." He palms the underside of my right thigh. "Relax, bunny. I'll do all the work."

And he thrusts inside.

~

JAEGER

SHE'S SOFT AND WARM. I steady her on the countertop, which is the perfect height for me.

Her pussy squeezes my cock. In no time, she has stars in her dark eyes. I lift her lush bottom right off the marble and pump into her.

Her complaint dies with a moan. "Ooooh."

"Yes, that's it. Cum for me." I kiss her forehead until she tips her head back and I can reach her lips. I was careful to step onto a bath mat so my feet won't slip.

It's been almost twenty-four hours since I've had her, and I can't go another minute. I'm going to fuck her often, I decide. Several times a day. She'll need food and rest to keep up, but time will increase her stamina. She'll live here and want for nothing.

I'll tell her soon. She seems confused about why she's here. I should be kind and ease her in, but I'm going as slowly as I can. I want her in my life, in my bed, for always.

I want her to be mine.

My balls tighten, and I slap my hips harder against hers. Her inner muscles clench on my cock. My hands are occupied, holding her suspended in the air, so I don't have a hand free to find her clit, but I angle my hips so my lower belly rubs her the right way. She gasps, shuddering with an orgasm. I keep pounding into her, my own orgasm rising.

Her arms are around my neck, squeezing tight. Her beautiful breasts rub my chest. But it's the way she curls into me, clinging like I'm her lifeline, that sends me over.

I want to be her rock in the storm. Her everything. She's the only one who has ever thanked me. She kissed me, and for a blissful second, I was a hero.

I want more.

But there's one obstacle to me claiming Elodie. I've sworn an oath to Fraternitas, and we're no ordinary brotherhood. I'll need the approval of the Devil and my brothers before I officially claim her. I need to do this right. I am a loyal soldier, but I won't tolerate anyone taking Elodie from me.

Nothing will stop me from possessing my sweet prey.

∼

ELODIE

FOR THE SECOND day in a row, I'm eating breakfast in bed with the man who paid to chase and fuck me in the woods. This time, I have no idea why.

"What are you doing?" I ask. I'm naked in bed, propped up against the pillows. Jaeger's in jeans and nothing else, with a tray of food on his lap.

"Feeding you." Intense with concentration, Jaeger scoops

up some scrambled eggs and carefully guides the fork to my mouth. "Open."

I squirm at the humiliation of being fed like a baby but give in and obey. I chew and swallow so I can keep questioning him. "I mean, why am I here? In your home... penthouse?" This place is amazing, but it doesn't feel like a home. It's nice, but there's zero personality. The first thing I'd do if I lived here is buy some knickknacks and throw pillows, maybe an indoor fern.

"Because I want you here." His lips quirk upward. "And you're hurt, so you can't leave."

I growl deep in my throat.

"Did you just growl at me? Bunny..." he says with so much fondness I want to punch him. He's moved himself up my People I Want to Kill list. He's not at the top, but the day is young.

"Do you want to go back to your apartment?" he asks.

I don't, of course, but I can't admit that to him. He'll use it as an argument to convince me to stay.

And why? What does he want with me? Other than fuck me and then feed me breakfast while I'm naked and he's not?

I'm afraid to ask outright.

I narrow my eyes at him. "Aren't you afraid you'll go down for murder? For the two guys?"

"What guys?" He frowns as he spreads strawberry jam on a fluffy-looking biscuit.

"The ones you threw down the stairs." Watching him wipe those men out was the most intense moment of my life. Chilling... and a little thrilling. But apparently, Jaeger's already forgotten it.

"No." He scoffs and feeds me the biscuit. I should be freaking out right now because Jaeger not only committed a double homicide in front of me but is shrugging it off completely. And it looks like the cops will, too.

Instead, I'm eating the softest buttery biscuit I've ever had right from his hand. I don't know where he found Southern-style biscuits in New Rome, but I could kiss him for it.

Again. But he'd get the wrong idea.

Again.

"What if Mr. Wilson talks—"

"He won't talk. He won't do anything. Neither will anyone else." He wipes crumbs away from my face with a napkin and leans in to kiss the side of my mouth. His lips taste sweet, so I must have had some strawberry jam clinging to mine. The kiss quickly deepens, his tongue sweeping into my mouth, and I'm lost in the waves, going under—

I plant my hands on his bare chest and push. I can't budge him, but it gets his attention.

"This is supposed to be over. I fulfilled the contract." I wave at my chest, which is bare because the blankets have slipped. "You got yours, so—"

He cups the back of my neck. "I want to take care of you."

That shuts me up. I let him go back to kissing me because I can't breathe. I've never had anyone say that to me. He sounds determined.

Just when I think he's going to push the blankets aside and fuck me again, he leans back and leaves the bed to clear the breakfast tray.

"I'm not in the market for a boyfriend," I tell him warily when he returns.

"Good. I'm not a boy." He gives me a dangerous smile. A

thrill runs through my body because my pussy is stupid when it comes to him.

I sigh. "Then when do I get my money?" If Jaeger insists I stay with him, I will until my ankle's a bit more healed. Then, I can use the money I earned to escape.

"Today." He pulls out his phone and starts texting. "I'll make the arrangements. St. James should be back in the city by now."

I stiffen because St. James is the scariest guy I've ever met. The fact that he wears expensive suits only makes him more intimidating. I've survived working at a business run by Fraternitas by keeping my head down. St. James is my boss's boss's boss, and I knew instinctively that I shouldn't attract his attention.

But now I've attracted Jaeger's, for better or worse. And while my ankle heals, I'm stuck with him. I might as well go with it and use this time to plan my escape.

"He says the money's ready for you at Inferno. We can go together to pick it up."

"What?" I was told the money would be deposited into my account. I'm not going to push back against a man like St. James, but I blanch at the thought of returning to my place of work with a hurt ankle and Jaeger at my side. "What am I going to wear?"

And that's how I find myself getting carried into a high end fashion shop, the sort Margot's model friends would work at while they tried to make it big.

"You need to stop doing this," I complain, even as I wind an arm around his neck to steady myself in his arms. Shoppers turn and stare at us.

"You can't walk." He doesn't seem to mind my grousing. He just looks amused. "And you said you needed clothes."

I'm wearing the joggers I wore yesterday and one of

Jaeger's shirts. It's huge on me, so I knotted it in the back. "I thought that was your plan. Keep me naked," I mutter.

"That's still my plan. I figured you would prefer this."

I shut up because of all the options, this is the best one. It's not a great idea to return to my apartment, and I didn't take any of my stuff. Not that I have anything worth taking. Everything I own could fit into a suitcase, and I'd be fine if I had to leave it all behind.

I didn't expect Jaeger to head straight to an exclusive shop on 5th Avenue. With his tattooed sleeves, he'd attract attention even if he wasn't carrying me bridal-style through the fancy store.

Over by a jewelry display, three skeletally thin ladies turn and stare. One of the ladies has a tiny dog in her purse, and it starts barking as Jaeger passes. He turns his head and gives the dog a long, hard look until it cringes. The ladies gasp and scuttle away.

The salespeople freeze when Jaeger approaches. "She needs clothes," he tells them. I wave hello and cross my arms over my chest.

The head salesperson glances down at Jaeger's skull ring and flies into action. "Oh, uh, yes... yes, of course."

In no time, I'm settled into a comfy armchair and given a glass of champagne. Jaeger takes point, standing beside me and ordering the staff around. Clothing piles up around me. I feel like Cinderella, but instead of a fairy godmother, I got a giant, scary godfather.

"That too." Jaeger points to a nearby mannequin displaying a slinky cocktail gown in white sequins, and I have to speak up.

"I do not need a dress," I argue. "Besides, that won't fit me."

"We'll have it fitted," the salesperson assures me. "We just need your measurements."

I open my mouth to say, "I can't afford that," but Jaeger speaks first. "Good. Take the measurements."

The salesperson's eyes light up. "And undergarments, what are we thinking?"

Jaeger turns to me, silencing me with his heated stare. "Lingerie. Lots of it."

"This is ridiculous," I say when I'm back in his arms, being carried out of the shop and wearing a brand-new outfit. Jaeger paid for everything. I didn't ask how much it cost, but the head salesperson had a big smile on her face when she promised to have the bags delivered to his penthouse.

Outside, the shop windows reflect the sight of Jaeger carrying me. I look good in my new vegan leather skirt and off-the-shoulder sweater. Jaeger is sexy in a black leather jacket, but he always looks sexy.

The worst part about him carrying me is how good he smells. And I'm up close and personal with his perfect profile, the golden stubble on his high cheekbones. Even though I've only known him for two days, my body is primed and ready. I'm soaking my new lace thong.

"We need to stop and get crutches," I argue. "You can't carry me everywhere."

"Yes, I can."

He's certainly strong enough.

"This isn't practical. I'll tell Atticus. He'll agree with me."

"Atticus can't see you until tonight. There was an emergency at the fight club."

I bite my top lip. The underground fight club is something Fraternitas is famous for. File it under stuff I don't want to know.

"You just like carrying me."

"You're right, bunny." He smiles with such warmth I have to look away.

Up ahead is a popular department store. "At least take me there to buy some more makeup," I grumble to distract myself from him.

"You don't need it," he says, but he makes the detour.

"Yeah, but your place could use some throw pillows." I point to a display in the home goods section.

He halts, staring at the display. "What is their purpose?"

I roll my eyes. "They make things homey. Have you seen where you live? I've been in corporate lobbies with more personality."

He sets me down in an armchair and waves over a sales associate. "Pick what you want."

"Are you serious?"

In answer, he picks up two candles. One is pine-scented, and the other reads 'spiced apple cider.' "Red or green?" he asks.

In the end, we get both candles, a bunch of throw pillows, and knickknacks. It's weird to decorate for a Fraternitas enforcer, so I pretend I'm window shopping with Margot.

Jaeger's penthouse is going to look like my favorite hygge magazine when I'm done with it. Will he look at it and remember me when I'm gone?

I can't think about that right now.

After the home goods section and make up counter, I raise my arms for Jaeger to lift me. "I think we've done enough damage for today. I'll pay you back for the makeup."

"No, you won't." He leans in and nuzzles my neck, smelling the perfume sample I tried.

I shiver, and the tingles spread through my core. "Stop it," I whisper.

"Stop what?" His lips ghost past my ear. "This?" He bows his head and kisses the spot where my pulse is pounding.

I turn my head. Unfortunately, we're in the jewelry section of the store, and I spy a ring that makes me gasp.

"What is it?" Jaeger raises his head, as alert as ever.

"Nothing," I say. But I can't take my eyes off the ring. It's made of delicate rose gold, with tiny, tear-shaped diamonds surrounding a pink center stone.

He moves us closer. "That one?" He studies the display.

I can't say anything. I've never seen anything so beautiful.

"Can I help you, sir?" an attendant asks.

"She wants to try that ring." Jaeger nods to it.

"No, I don't." I curl my hands into fists. I'm close to crying for some reason.

The attendant is already taking the ring out of the display case. "Are you sure, Miss?"

"Just try it…" Jaeger tips me so I can offer my hand. The salesman slides it on my ring finger.

It fits perfectly.

"Beautiful," the salesman gushes.

"I don't want it," I whisper. I pull off the ring and hand it back.

Jaeger just responds with a "Hmmm." I keep my eyes fixed on the black shapes of his tattoos swirling out front under his collar.

After a moment, he moves on. I breathe a sigh when he carries me out of the shop.

"Lunchtime," he announces. I don't say anything. I'm trying to unravel my freak-out in the shop. I'm mostly fine with Jaeger literally carrying me off to his home, treating me like I'm helpless, buying me anything I need. Fixing my problems. Fucking me anyway he wants.

What is it about me that I just accept this, but when I see something that I want, I freeze up in fear for no reason? Am I so ground down by life that all I can do is keep my head down, going from problem to problem and just trying to survive?

Will I ever have the courage to reach for what I really want?

7

E *lodie*

WHEN JAEGER CARRIES me into the shadow-filled foyer of Inferno, the black-haired hostess with a ruby-jeweled nose ring does a double take.

"Elodie?" My friend's eyes widen when she sees who's carrying me.

"Hi, Daria." I give her a little wave.

She gulps as Jaeger approaches and grabs two menus. "This way, sir." Her tone is brisk and professional, but she glances back a few times while leading us through the club.

"Did we have to come here?" I whisper to him.

"You want to get paid."

"Yeah, but I haven't told my boss I'm going to be MIA for a few days." In all the excitement, I forgot to call in. I was hoping to explain and maybe swap shifts with a hostess who can also wait tables. I can work if I can sit down the whole time.

"That's all handled."

"What do you mean?

"St. James knows about your ankle."

I suck in a breath. Getting on St. James' radar is NOT what I want. I want to ask what else he knows about me, but I also don't want to know.

Inferno is divided into two areas. Up front are steakhouse-style booths and mahogany-paneled private rooms. It's lunch hour, so this part of the restaurant is packed.

In the back is the gentleman's club. I don't work back there unless it's super slammed. I know there are secret poker games, gambling, and illegal dealings of all kinds that happen at all hours.

Today, there are a few groups doing business at the round tables, ignoring the burlesque dancer on stage. I wave to the dancer, Angel, as I pass. She waves her white feather fan and winks at me.

Daria guides us back through the club all the way to the VIP area above the dancers' stage. I've waited tables in the front of Inferno and the dancers' area, but I've never been up here before.

This area is reserved for Fraternitas members.

Daria stops at a central booth set against the wall. "How's this?"

"Fine." Jaeger sets me down, and I scoot deep into the circular seat.

Two tattooed guys sit at the bar. They have to be Fraternitas if they're in the VIP area. Sure enough, both wear skull rings on their middle fingers. Jaeger gives them a nod.

"I'll be right back." He digs his hand into my hair and tugs my head back, kissing the heck out of me. I'm gasping into his mouth before he drags his lips down to my collar-bone and sucks hard enough to bruise.

Then he's gone, and I'm rubbing the wet spot he left on my skin. It's probably bright red. A claiming mark.

Stealthy as a shadow, Daria slides into the booth in his place. She leans close, the jewel in her nose ring glittering. "Girl, what is going on?"

I'm still catching my breath. "It's a long story."

"So tell me," she hisses. A shadow falls over the table, and we straighten, only to see it's another waitress, Honey.

"What are you guys doing?" she asks, and we hush her.

"Elodie is here... with someone." Daria bounces her eyebrows.

"Like..." Honey's gaze darts to the thugs at the bar. "One of them? Which one?"

"His name is Jaeger," I say.

"Oooh," Honey murmurs. "He's fine. So is his brother. Have you met Kaiser yet?"

"No." I didn't even know Jaeger had a brother.

"He's scary. Scary hot." Honey pretends to swoon.

"Come on, girl." Daria raps the table. "Spill. You have thirty seconds before Lucy catches us." Lucy is the head manager of Inferno and rules with an iron fist. She can be more intimidating than all the Fraternitas members combined.

"Lucy will forgive us," Honey says. "She likes you."

"No, she doesn't," Daria shoots back without taking her eyes off me.

"She does," Honey insists. It's an old argument, one they've happily bickered about in snatches of conversation between serving customers.

I scoot to the edge of the booth. "Help me up. I want to go to the ladies' room."

"What happened to your ankle?" Daria asks, but she and Honey come on either side of me and help me hobble down the hall.

We enter the spacious bathroom. There's a lounge area next to the stalls, and I drop into one of the chairs.

"Tell us everything," Daria demands.

I feel warm and fuzzy facing them. Once I dropped out of college and started working here, my life became nothing but sleeping and double shifts with a side of babysitting for Margot. I've been too tired to do anything for myself, much less chase the friends I made in college.

I never meant for my co-workers to become my closest friends, but that's how life goes. Where you spend your time becomes your home. The people around you become your community. Once I made the choice to work at Inferno, all the other choices cascaded from here, and my destiny was set.

But looking at Daria and Honey, I realize how much I need their friendship. We share gossip and blister pads and complain about long shifts and stingy tippers. Their support is all I have, and because of that, it means the world.

So I tell them my story, starting with St. James' offer and ending with the shopping spree, but I keep my freak-out over the ring to myself. The ladies ooh and ahh at appropriate places, and when I'm done, Daria's tapping her chin, deep in thought.

"St. James doesn't make that offer to just anyone," she says. "Not to any waitresses or dancers, at least, because one of them would talk, and I would've found out. That means Jaeger singled you out."

Honey gasps. "Because he wants you. You've been chosen." She gives me a dazzling smile.

"What?" I ask.

"You know, one of them," Honey says and then adds in a whisper, "An *elita*."

I glance at Daria, but neither of us has any idea what Honey's talking about.

"What's an *elita*?" Daria folds her arms in front of her chest.

"One of the chosen." Honey sees our confusion and rolls her eyes. "You guys have to start paying attention."

"Paying attention can get us killed," Daria grumbles, and I concur.

"Whatever," Honey says. "Remember Odette?"

The name sounds familiar, but I don't remember her until Daria says, "The dancer? She worked here for, like, a hot second."

"Right. And now she only comes in on the arm of that big guy with the neck tattoo. The one with jewels in his ring," Honey lowers her voice again. "One of the Seven."

I don't know what she means by 'one of the Seven,' and I don't want to know. But I remember Odette. "She came in a few weeks ago with him," I say slowly. "She was wearing a black ribbon around her throat with a blue jewel on it."

"Right, to match his ring." Honey rolls her hands in a "ta-da" gesture and sighs when we still look confused. "She's an initiate. That's what you become before the ceremony when you're claimed."

Ceremony? I have so many questions, but I feel like I've been tromping through the woods, only to come to a fence covered in barbed wire and a *No Trespassing* sign.

Daria looks skeptical. "How do you know so much about this?"

Honey flushes and examines her French manicure. "I just do."

"Okay," I say, "So what? Some of the Fraternitas claim their elite—"

"*Elita*. Or *Electus*, if they're male," Honey corrects and sticks her tongue out at Daria, who's shaking her head.

"*Elita*." I can't shake the feeling of dread like I shouldn't know this term. "What does that have to do with Jaeger?"

"Everything." Honey crouches in front of me and takes my hands in hers. "The reason you're here—in a booth and not working the floor—is because Jaeger wants to claim you."

"He can't claim me. I'm not, not..." My brain is blanking like it did when I tried on the ring. *Danger! Turn back!* "This isn't like that."

"He brought you here to show you off in front of Fraternitas. He wants to claim you as his *elita*."

"What would that entail?" Daria asks.

"I don't know. The ritual is kept secret. Like everything about Fraternitas. I can try to get in touch with Odette—"

"No, don't." I shake my head.

"It's like the skull rings," Honey says. "They earn them by killing a man. Or is it ten?"

I get a violent flashback to Jaeger in the stairwell, the blood spattered on his jaw.

"Oh, gods." I lean over my knees. "I don't want to know."

"Elodie," Daria says, and I cover my ears with my hands. Not that I can hear anything over the loud rushing sound, like water crashing through a hole in a giant dam. I close my eyes.

When I open them again, Honey and Daria are looking at me sympathetically.

"I'm sure it'll turn out okay," Honey says. She squeezes my knee and stands.

"We have to get back to work." Daria motions to Honey to leave and hesitates, looking back at me.

"Go," I say. "I need a minute." I have to calm down before I can face Jaeger and a roomful of men with skull rings.

Daria hesitates again, and I flap a hand at her. "I'll be fine." I knot my hands together until the door shuts, and I'm alone.

My ankle is sore but nowhere near as painful as it was yesterday. A good night's sleep helped a ton. Maybe I'll be mobile sooner than later.

And then what? Can I run? Where do I go? I can't head to Aunt Carol's. Besides not wanting to lead the loan sharks there, her hospitality will be stretched too thin. Better for me to run in the opposite direction.

Another thought hits me. Jaeger knows where Margot is. He could threaten her and the kids or hold them over my head as blackmail to make me return.

I reject the thought as soon as I have it. Jaeger will never hurt her or the kids. I don't know him well, but I know that.

He has an odd sense of honor for a murdering criminal.

But I'm afraid Honey is right. Jaeger might want to keep me. And nothing will stop him.

There are murmurs in the hallway outside the door, and I figure I've been in here long enough.

I grab the chair rail and use it to support my slow limp to the door. Once I'm there, I lean on the handle, shifting my weight, and open it.

There's a dark figure in the hall. I startle back until the low light gleams on a golden head.

"Jaeger?" All I can see of him is a tattooed hand and a skull ring.

When the figure steps into the light, I realize it's not Jaeger at all.

The man looks like Jaeger, with the same leonine head and stormy blue eyes. His face is identical, and even the tattoos are similar. But he's not the same. This isn't the man I ran from in the forest or the one I snuggled with last night.

No, this man looks down on me like I'm a bug he's about to squash. Jaeger has never looked at me like this.

"Who are you?" My question dies on my lips when he steps forward. A big hand, covered to the knuckle with a spiderweb tattoo, cups my jaw. He turns my face this way and that.

A jolt of fear runs through me at his callous touch. I freeze like a rabbit in a trap.

Before I collect myself to scream or push him away, he releases me and steps back, a sneer twisting his face.

"So, little red," he says. "You're the one who's trapped my brother."

8

E *lodie*

I GAPE AT THE BLOND. He looks so much like his brother, it's disconcerting. *Identical twins.* Like Jaeger, he's scarily hot. But while Jaeger inspires comfort and lust, this man, with the same face, only makes me feel terror. I'm shaking as I lean against the wall outside the bathroom.

"What do you have to say for yourself?" He's standing too close. Jaeger's up in my space all the time, but I've gotten used to it. I even long for it, whereas my body reads this guy as a pure, unadulterated threat. We're in a dark hallway where only fellow members of Fraternitas will hear a cry for help.

"Hmm?" Jaeger's brother prompts.

"I didn't." I squeak. Me, trap Jaeger? More like the other way around. But how can I explain that to him? Fear is twisting my stomach so much I want to puke.

He lifts a hand, and I cringe, only for him to stroke the gold stubble on his chin. His skull ring sits prominently on his middle finger. The shadows in the eye sockets go down forever.

"Kaiser." Jaeger appears at the end of the hall.

I can't stop the forceful flood of relief at the sight of him loping toward me. He lifts me into his arms, and I cling to him. Kaiser glares at me, but I'm safe in his brother's arms. I have the feeling that the only reason he hasn't snapped my neck and left me for dead is because Jaeger is here. It makes me grip Jaeger tighter.

"This is Elodie," Jaeger says. "Elodie, this is my brother, Kaiser."

Kaiser and I say nothing to each other.

"She should not be here," Kaiser tells Jaeger while still staring at me like he hopes his gaze will incinerate me. I don't even try to stare him down. A rabbit can't stare down a wolf.

"She's with me."

Kaiser transfers his glare to his brother. There's another intense staring match. This time, the opponents are equally matched. I can only hope the twin holding me wins.

"She belongs here," Jaeger says, and it unsettles me. I feel like he's talking about more than us having lunch here this one time.

"We'll see," Kaiser says and walks away. His shadow stretches down the corridor. At the end, he slams a door.

Well, that's not ominous at all.

"Are you all right?"

I clutch him harder. I've never been the intense object of hate of someone I've just met.

"It's all right. Kaiser would never hurt you."

I can't be so sure.

Back at the booth, our table is full of food. I sit and wring my hands as Jaeger inhales a steak the size of a dinner plate.

"You're not eating." He frowns and pushes a dish of mashed potatoes my way.

I shrug.

"Here." He leans down and grabs a black briefcase, sliding it across the table. "This will make you feel better."

I open it, half expecting to see plastic baggies filled with tempting little pills. Instead, it's stacks and stacks of hundred-dollar bills.

"What is this?" I ask stupidly. I have the crazy feeling I should snap the case shut and hide it in case the Feds are watching our illicit trade.

"Your payment."

I do some mental math, but my mind blanks. This is way more than ten thousand dollars.

"One hundred thousand," Jaeger says helpfully. "You can count it. St. James won't be offended."

St. James. Right, that shark is involved in all this. The less time he spends thinking of me, the better.

I close the briefcase and push it away. "I didn't make it until dawn."

"Didn't you?" He smiles when I stare at him.

Does he mean, 'Did I survive him?' I guess I did. I lived until dawn. He didn't kill me and leave me in the woods.

I know, deep down, that had been an option. But somehow, I've avoided that fate. In that sense, I did earn the money.

All of a sudden, I'm not afraid anymore. I'm mad.

I take the briefcase and set it at my side, holding his gaze the whole time. "With this money, I could leave you."

"You could try," he murmurs. "You wouldn't get far. You're hurt, remember?"

"I won't always be hurt." This is reckless, but I'm past caring. I feel the same way I had in that moment in the woods, when I was sick of running and stopped to challenge him.

"You're right. You'll heal up fast." He leans close enough that I can pick out the dark striations in his stormy eyes. "That's when you'll find out if you take more than a few steps away from me, I'll hunt you down. And you know how good I am at hunting."

My heart trips and adrenaline careens through my body, flipping every switch to give it a turbo boost of energy. But my pussy thinks it's go-time. Jaeger's lips are close to mine, his wintry scent suffusing my lungs. Arousal pounds in my core, leaving me soaked.

"You can't get away," Jaeger taunts, a happy look on his flawless face. He looks almost angelic with his serene smile and gilt hair.

"Fuck you," I say loud enough for the men at the bar to turn.

Jaeger's blue eyes light up. "Definitely. That was always the plan."

~

JAEGER

MY BUNNY REFUSES to talk to me the whole way home. I thought she'd be happy at being handed such a healthy sum of money, but it only brought more worries.

She's used to worrying. Life has not been kind to her. I hope to be a shield for her, a safe place in the storm.

I carry her into my penthouse, ready to strip her down and fuck her. A nice, hard fuck always makes her feel better.

As soon as the lights come on, illuminating the apartment, she gasps. There are a few new additions to the place, starting with two blooming orchids on pedestal stands on either side of the entryway.

"Where did these come from?" I pause to let her touch one of the orchid's soft purple petals.

"Do you like them?" She said she wanted to make changes to the penthouse. I paid the shop to send their best decorator along with the home goods purchases she made. The decorator had free reign to add a few of their own touches as well.

Judging by the awestruck look on Elodie's face, it was worth it.

"They're beautiful." I wait until she's looked her fill and carry her into the living space. The space is transformed. There are more plants—ferns and shit like that—placed in corners, and scented candles cast a soft light over the space. The three throw pillows Elodie picked out are arranged on the couch, with more throw pillows on each chair and fuzzy blankets draped over the arms of the chairs.

Elodie's eyes are alight. I set her down, and she clutches a pillow to her chest, taking it all in. "When did all this happen?"

"While we were at lunch. I had the shop deliver it."

She wrinkles her nose. "How?"

I drop a kiss on her forehead. She's too adorable. "Money." Money can do anything. "Do you like it?"

"I do."

Her mood seems lighter, so I squeeze the back of her neck, holding her still as I claim her lips. *This is all for you.* I need to tell her that she can make any changes she likes. *This is your home now.*

A text, followed by a rap on the door, tells me Atticus is outside. I let him in and bring him to Elodie. I'm still carrying the briefcase full of Elodie's cash, so I leave them to it and head to my nearest safe. I have many of them around the penthouse and more scattered throughout the city, filled with caches of weapons, jewels, alternate identities, and money in several denominations.

"I meant to come this morning, but there was an emergency," Atticus is telling Elodie.

"It's fine." She holds out her arm and lets him swab it for a shot. He convinced her to allow him to give her an infusion of vitamins and painkillers, a healing cocktail of his own design.

I sense her gaze on me and turn to show her the safe hidden behind some wall paneling. "The password is your birthday." I set the briefcase inside. She can access it at any time.

If she uses it to escape me, she won't get far, but it will ease her mind to know it's there.

When she's more settled, I'll show her the options she can invest in. St. James runs several hedge funds under different shell companies. He's the reason Fraternitas has real wealth. With his help, the brotherhood has been transformed from a back alley gang to a real power in the city with diverse and legitimate enterprises. He's structured the organization so everyone in Fraternitas shares in the profits, which makes us all multi-millionaires.

St. James can do the same for her. Investing in his companies will increase her savings to a few million in just a few years.

But there'll be time to explain all that. My bunny is skittish in her new habitat and needs time to adjust.

I sink onto the couch next to Elodie, careful not to jostle her. As she and Atticus talk, I play with her curls.

"I still recommend you stay off the ankle," Atticus says. "It's looking better, but you're not out of the woods yet."

Elodie's shoulders tense. "What about work?"

"I talked to Lucy," I interrupt. Lucy runs Inferno. "She'll hold your job until you're healed." After I claim Elodie, she'll have no need for a job, but she seems friendly with the other waitresses. I don't want to disrupt her whole life or interfere with her relationships.

I just want to be the only man in her life. And make her happy.

Elodie frowns. "You had no right," she says.

"Lucy likes me. And you seemed stressed about it. I thought I'd explain things for you."

She sighs but doesn't say any more. She's starting to learn how it'll be from now on: when life is rocky, I'll do anything to clear obstacles out of her way.

"Sounds like you have the all-clear to rest and heal," Atticus says. "Avoid any activities that would stress your ankle."

"What about sex?" I ask him while watching my bunny closely.

Elodie's mouth falls open, and a flush creeps over her freckled cheeks.

Atticus is unruffled. He treats all manner of wounds, from the fight club members to the dancers at Inferno, not to mention the club submissives at the Lodge and St. James' other BDSM club, Club Empire. "Sex is fine."

I'm enjoying the ripe red glow of Elodie's blush, so I add, "Anything we should avoid? Like spanking?"

"That's between you and her." Atticus gives me a level look. "As far as I'm concerned, she can spank you as much as you like."

Ha. Ha. I give him a cold smile. He smirks, tossing a bunch of condoms on the coffee table, along with a few packets of lube. "Have fun," he says. I walk him to the door and lock the door behind him before prowling back to Elodie's side.

She's frowning again. "We need to talk."

I pounce. "Later." I strip off her sweater before she can fight me. "I'm going to make you feel good."

"Jaeger," she growls, and I kiss her neck, feeling her pulse jump under my lips. Thumbing her nipples through her new satin bra, she shivers. I plant kisses from her throat to her breastbone and stroke her soft belly.

"I've missed this." I unzip the side of her skirt and peel it down enough to release her scent. Her perfume blooms around me, making my mouth water.

"Missed what? We've been together." She gives me a surly look. "All day."

"My bunny doesn't like change." I kiss between her breasts and scrape my stubbled chin on her tender skin until she squirms. "She needs to feel safe."

"I don't know what you're talking about."

"No?" I rise and pull a small velvet pouch out of my pocket. I shake the ring she wanted into my palm, and she gasps. I take her hand and slide it onto her left ring finger.

I've never cared for tradition or ceremony, but there's something satisfying about collaring her in this way. The pink stone gives off a subtle gleam in the setting of sparkling diamonds. *Mine.*

"You bought it." She's awestruck again, staring at the ring.

I shrug. "You wanted it." What my woman wants, she gets.

She fiddles with the ring as if she's reluctant to accept it but likes the look of it too much to remove it. She clutches her hand to her chest and worries her lip. "I can pay you back."

I rear back. "No." I glower at her, offended she would offer. "You're my woman. You don't pay for anything. Ever."

"I'm... your woman?" Her brow furrows. She's back to twisting the ring around her finger, thinking hard. "Is this payment?"

"What?"

She holds up her hand, showing off the ring. "Is this my payment for sleeping with you again?"

Anger suffuses my chest so quickly I'm speechless.

She raises her chin. "What will I get if I spend the night? Another ten thousand dollars?"

"I'm not paying you," I grind out. "I'm not hiring you."

"Then—"

"You are my woman." I take her hand and check the ring, making sure it's secure. Her soft hand in mine calms me. I press a kiss to her palm and release it. "Ask for anything, and it's yours."

She blinks a few times. "Like the throw pillows." She lifts one to demonstrate.

"Yes."

Her eyes narrow. "Helping my sister. Making sure she and the kids are safe. And that she has her meds."

I nod. "Done."

"And this ring. You think this makes me yours."

"You are mine." I set my hand at the base of her throat. "I'm not asking. You don't have a choice in this, baby." I lean close enough to hear the catch in her breath. To smell the sweetness of her sex as she starts to cream for me. "But I will make it good for you. You'll want for nothing from now on."

ELODIE

I STARE into Jaeger's eyes, glittering more brilliantly than any jewel.

He bought the ring. He bought the ring!

"I'm not for sale," I blurt, desperate.

"I'm not buying you." The weight of his hand around my throat is comforting. "I've claimed you. You're already mine."

He wants to claim you. Honey had told me, but I didn't want to listen. *He wants you to be his* elita.

Newsflash, Honey, he thinks it's already happened.

He's upset at my confusion. As if my being here, belonging to him, was a foregone conclusion.

Today he took me shopping and bought everything I'd need for a life with him. I mentioned once that I didn't like his home, and he redecorated everything. Immediately.

He's acting like we're a couple already. On some level, I knew this. It's likely why I got weirded out by the ring.

But then he gave me a briefcase with a hundred thousand dollars for services rendered. My eyes dart to the wall panel where he put my money in the safe.

He follows my gaze and my line of thinking. "The payment was for one night, an exchange between two independent parties. There'll be no more payouts. We are no longer independent parties. We are one."

I shake my head slightly, and his hand tightens until I can't move. I'm the poor, helpless prey caught in a trap.

"You're not independent, little red. You're mine."

9

E^{lodie}

I LAY IN BED, icing my ankle. Since Atticus's visit a few days ago, the swelling has gone way down, but I'm still taking pain meds and icing it. Keeping to the routine and staying off of it so I can heal.

There isn't much else for me to do. With Margot and the kids safe, I don't have to scramble to survive. I'm so used to going from one crisis to the next that I have no idea what to do with myself except worry about me and Jaeger.

You're my woman. Just like that, I belong to him.

What would it be like to be so certain? So sure?

We've settled into an uneasy truce. He seems to sense I need time to digest this. He's left me alone to eat delicious food—he has some sort of meal service set up for his pent-house because whatever I'm in the mood for shows up on a covered tray within minutes—and lounge around the cozy living room watching rom-coms.

The ring sparkles on my hand. Every time I look at it, I want to hyperventilate, but I don't take it off.

This can't last. Men always leave. I might as well get what I can out of this crazy arrangement before he gets tired of having me around.

If that makes me a gold digger, so be it.

Jaeger disappears for most of the day, which I'm grateful for at first but also resent. He doesn't have a traditional nine-to-five sort of day job but lurks around, taking phone calls, then coming and going at all hours. It leaves me to wonder what he's up to. What does he do for Fraternitas? All the evidence points to him being an enforcer for the brother-hood, which means blood and violence. I spiral on this before telling myself I don't want to know.

He does take every opportunity to kiss, eat, or fuck me. To the point where I get wet when he walks into the room.

This afternoon is no exception. I wake from a nap to the door opening.

"Honey, I'm home." Jaeger prowls to my side and kisses me before I realize I'm not dreaming about a Viking marauder breaking into my fantasy hygge home to ravage me. His golden stubble scrapes my cheeks, and the prickly sensation wakes me up.

Before I know it, I'm wrapping my arms around him and sliding my hands under his shirt and up his back. There's a rough edge under my palm. His brand. I realize what I'm touching and yank my hand away.

"Where were you?" I ask before I remember that's not a great question to ask a mafia thug.

"Out. Did you eat?" He sifts through the remnants of my

lunch and frowns when he finds a whole club sandwich. I nibbled on one piece of bacon and ate the tomato soup and chips instead.

"You're not eating enough," he accuses me and wolfs down half the sandwich in one bite.

I brush crumbs off my sweatshirt so I don't completely look like a poster child for depression. "I'm fine."

"You need your strength." He studies my ankle and squeezes my bare knee. I've taken to wearing skirts and dresses to make it easy to dress and undress. At his innocuous touch, heat runs up my bare leg, and my pussy begins to throb. "You need all your strength to handle me."

My body is heating up, ready to *handle* him.

I cross my arms over my chest. "You're not the boss of me."

"No?" He finishes the sandwich and gives me a wolfish smile that makes my breasts swell.

To hide my reaction, I growl at him.

"Grumpy bunny." He climbs over me, pressing me into the couch cushions and nuzzling my face. My hips rise automatically to meet him. "It's okay. I know how to make you sweet." He's going to fuck me again and leave me dazed and pliant from orgasms. And my body is ready for it.

I push at his shoulder. "Stop."

He grabs my palm and kisses it. "You don't want me to fuck you? To suck your clit until you're screaming my name?"

I suck in a breath. I do want all that. I've had it before, earlier today and three times yesterday, and my clit remembers it fondly. He fights dirty.

He props himself up, his hips still pressing into my pulsing core. His weight is delicious, and I want more, but he takes a moment to cup my cheek in one huge hand. "You like me, bunny. Why do you resist this?"

Out of the corner of my eye, I see his skull ring. I'm used to seeing it, and I shouldn't be. It should still inspire a thrill of fear.

I bite my lip.

"Are you stressed?" He's peering at me.

"Of course, I'm stressed. I'm twenty-two and have spent most of my life completely broke. What broke twenty-something isn't a stress bucket?"

"Can I fix it?"

I sigh. "Not today." Especially because he's what I'm worried about.

"Okay, bunny." He kisses my nose and lifts off of me. The loss of him makes me dizzy.

He walks to the kitchen, like everything's normal. I hit play on the movie I was watching before I paused it to take a nap. A minute later, Jaeger's back with a jumbo tin that turns out to be filled with three types of fancy popcorn.

He offers the tin to me first, and I take a handful, but I tense up when he settles on the couch next to me. I'm halfway through a bonkers rom-com set in a small town that celebrates Christmas all year. If Jaeger's like any of my old boyfriends, he's five seconds away from grabbing the remote and changing the channel so he can watch sportsball.

A minute passes. I hold my breath. On-screen, the winner of the Snow Queen beauty pageant is making a speech about saving the town.

Jaeger munches on popcorn, his blue eyes fixed on the screen. "Is this the one with the gingerbread-making contest?"

I blink at him. "What?"

"The movie. Is this the one with the gingerbread-making contest to save the small town? Or the one with the long-lost prince and widow?"

I look from him to the TV screen and back again. He seems serious. "There's one with a long-lost prince and a widow?"

"You haven't seen that one?" He points to the screen where a rugged lumberjack is yelling at a trio of kids dressed like elves, telling them that he hates Christmas. "That's the actor who plays the prince. They just had him shave his beard and dye his hair blond."

"Really?" The lumberjack looks good with his wild-man beard. I try to picture him as a clean-shaven blond, and the result is pretty bland. "Ugh."

"Yeah. He looks better like this." Jaeger takes another handful of popcorn and leans back, slinging his free arm behind me. "But there's a great ice skating routine. Let's watch the prince movie next."

What? I twist to stare at him. "You like these movies?"

He shrugs. "Who doesn't?"

"Most macho men wouldn't be caught dead watching stuff like this." I put my hand out, feeling for his crotch. My palm brushes a hard bulge in his jeans.

He raises a brow.

"Just checking to make sure you have a dick."

He grabs my wrist and presses my hand against him more firmly. "Oh, I have one. Want me to prove it?"

I shake my head, turning back to the screen. "Let's just watch the movie."

To my surprise, he does. We finish the movie, and he puts on the one with the blond prince. The plot is more ridiculous than the first and very satisfying.

About halfway through, he finishes the popcorn and goes to wash his hands. When he returns, he slips a hand on my belly and strokes my skin. I frown at him, and he smiles back.

He keeps fondling me through the final scenes, and, yes, the ice skating scene is epic. I start to shift in my seat, squirming under his touch. It's relentless and never moves below my waist.

Finally, the credits roll.

"Well?" I demand.

"Well, what?" He leans in to kiss me.

"You know what."

"Mmmm." He presses into me, shifting me until I'm on my back, and he's over me. I kiss him back, but he pauses. "You were stressed before. Tell me why."

Oh, now he wants to talk? I jerk my hips, trying to get his attention back on what we're doing.

He doesn't move but keeps watching me expectantly. Am I supposed to have a conversation with him on top of me?

"We shouldn't be together," I blurt. "We're not compatible."

He searches my eyes as if I'm holding back the real answer. "You're wrong. You're just afraid." He shifts his body slightly, and I shudder under his delicious weight. "You know we fit."

I push at him. I need space for this conversation. He rises as if I've muscled him off me, but I know I didn't because I'm not capable of physically forcing him to do anything.

I struggle to sit upright, and he helps me, then perches on the coffee table so he's close but not crowding me. He leans forward, the picture of a predator ready to pounce. His jeans are ripped, with white strands frayed across his knees.

The light streaming from the penthouse windows catches his stubble and makes it gleam like gold.

He's so hot he takes my breath away.

"I'm not afraid," I snap, and he raises a brow. "I'm not. It's just... we barely know each other."

"I know enough. The hunt, the chase. You liked it." His eyes glimmer with satisfaction. "You came hard enough on my cock."

At the word "cock," my eyes dart to the bulge in his jeans. Crap, he's still hard. Heat suffuses my chest.

I drag my eyes back to his face, where he's taking in my reactions. "Don't lie to me, bunny. You enjoyed being my prey."

Before I can think, I throw a pillow at him. Instantly, his blue gaze turns laser-focused. He launches himself onto the couch, pouncing.

I squeal and try to roll away, but he pins me easily. He presses his length into me, and my hips rise to meet his.

"I told you. You like this." He kisses the tip of my ear, sending tingles down my back. "You like baiting me." He kisses the side of my nose, where the most freckles are. He's obsessed with my freckles. One day, I'll cover them with makeup and see what he does.

"You like me." He forestalls my argument with a deep kiss. Heat blooms through me. Instead of pushing him away, I'm digging my fingers into his soft T-shirt, pulling him close. His scent rolls over me, that manly musk that drives me wild.

"Fuck you," I mutter against his mouth.

"Oh, I plan to."

He pulls up my dress and sees I'm not wearing undies. He hums in approval and tips me to my side so he can smack my ass.

"Ouch," I yelp, even though it didn't really hurt.

He rubs the sting away, and I bite back a moan.

"Fuck, Jaeger."

"Yes, bunny. Yes, I will fuck you." His fingers find the neck of my dress, and he rips it open. I gasp, and my breasts spill out. Today was a no-bra day.

"Yes," he breathes and dives in. His stubble rubs against my sensitive flesh, making me squirm. "You're so soft." He palms my stomach. He doesn't care that it's not toned and flat. He seems to love how the plush folds spill over his hands.

Every worshipful kiss rubs me raw. I make a pained noise, and he raises his head. "Did I hurt you?"

My stomach is red from the scratchy shadow of his beard. I cup his face. "Your stubble."

He starts to rise. "I can shave—"

"No." I pull him back. My pussy is weeping onto the couch cushions. I can't wait any longer.

"No?" His blue eyes hold mine. "I don't want to hurt you." He glances at my ankle. "You're fragile."

"It's okay." And it is because he's been caring for me. Any other guy would be history, but Jaeger won't leave. He won't let me leave, either.

Right now, that's what I need.

"I like it," I whisper, and this time, when I pull him back down, he dives in again. He rubs his jaw along my inner thighs, kissing my stretch marks and running his tongue over the silvery scars. I'm rolling my hips, desperate for relief by the time he drags his lips to my pussy. He eats me with abandon, thrusting his fingers into my wet channel, finding my G-spot and rubbing it until I'm about to shatter.

He stops before I reach the apex. I growl at him, but he rises up, stripping off his shirt, and the sight of his muscles flexing distracts me. His tattoos are dark swirling chaos, snakes and oceans, a shipwreck, a white-eyed god. A prowling wolf beside a blooming lotus flower. A blindfolded goddess. The total effect is stunning. He's a living, breathing work of art.

He pushes down his jeans just enough to free his hard, dripping cock. I lick my lips, my breath coming faster.

"You ready for me, bunny?" He jerks himself, his eyes on my weeping slit.

I slide down and spread my legs. He makes me weak. I need him to fill me and pound me into the couch until I'm mindless and all my worries are far away.

He sheathes himself inside me, and we both sigh. I wrap my left leg around his back, urging him to rest his weight on me. He's taller than me, so I end up tucked into his chest. Completely covered by him. Warm and safe.

When he's inside me, as close to me as a person can get, everything makes sense.

And when he moves, he drives every thought out of my noisy head. I brace myself against him. The ocean swirls before my eyes. The lotus flower wilts and blooms.

He slides a hand along my raised leg, hitching it higher. The angle catches my clit, and I go over, biting his nipple as I do. His pecs stiffen under my lips. With a roar, he finishes inside me.

But he's not fully finished.

He wraps his hand around my neck, drawing my head up. His back bows so he can kiss me, his lips dominating mine hard enough to bruise.

In no time, he's hard inside me.

"Again?"

"Again."

By the time he's done, the sun has set. The penthouse is

dark but for some flickering cider-scented candles. We lie together, tangled on the couch. I'm on my side, surrounded by him. Somehow, he's made sure my hurt ankle is propped on a pillow.

My thoughts drift back to me, one by one. I watch them float by and fade, the panic drained out of them.

You're my woman. When did he decide this? Was it the night he chased me? The morning after?

"You okay?" Jaeger sifts his fingers through my hair. I realize I've been staring at him with a frown on my face.

"I'm trying to understand you."

He grins. "I'm a simple man. I'm loyal to my brothers and protect my woman. What else is there to understand?"

"When did you know? That you wanted me. For, you know, this." He gazes at me, and I fight the urge to squirm. His cum is leaking out of me, but I'm avoiding direct reference to the "my woman" comment. "When did you decide you wanted me longer than a night?"

"When did I decide you were my woman?"

"Um." I do squirm a little. "Yes."

Satisfied, he leans back. "You were running from me. I could taste your fear, and I was hungry for it. But then, you got angry. You stopped and faced me."

I remember that moment. I'd thought it was all over. *Come get me,* I challenged him.

"I used to fight in the underground rings. I've faced many men. They all started out confident, but after a few blows, the pain would bleed their courage away until they were begging for the end."

I've heard rumors about the Fraternitas fight club, that some fights are to the death. I don't know if Jaeger participated in those fights, but right now, he's far away.

I palm his cheek to bring him back.

"You were different," he says. "You had no chance. But when your fear bled away, only you remained."

"So you wanted me... because I yelled at you?"

"Yes," he states. Like it's a simple equation that makes perfect sense.

"You don't even know me," I murmur, mostly to myself.

But Jaeger hears. He has the sharpened senses of a predator. "I want to know you."

I sigh.

"Let me know you," he whispers, taking my chin between two fingers so I can't escape his gaze.

Who is this man? He's covered in tattoos and has a skull branded into his back. He kills without remorse. Yet he watches rom-coms and loves to cuddle, and he wants to know me.

"All right," I say. I've decided on a test. "Take me somewhere tonight."

He rolls to a sitting position, carrying me with him. "Anywhere."

He says that now, but we'll see how long it lasts.

A half-hour later, he pulls up to the location. I gave him the address with no explanation so he wouldn't know where we were going until his Lykan purred up to the curb.

"A church?" he says, looking up at the cross affixed to the front of the modest brick building.

"What?" I taunt. "Are you worried you're going to catch fire if you enter?"

He smirks and turns off the car. Once again, he's illegally parked out front. It's like he has no regard for any laws.

He comes around to open my door to lift me out. "I was raised by a man of the cloth, bunny. This place doesn't scare me."

"Wait, you were?" I've accused him of not knowing me,

but I don't know much about him, either. "Where did you grow up?"

"On the streets of New Rome," he says so easily that I stiffen. "But not for Father Francis's lack of trying."

At my guidance, he carries me around the side of the building to the stairs leading to the basement where the Narcotics Anonymous meetings are held.

A trio of smokers stand off the path. They do double-takes at the sight of me and Jaeger, and I give them a wave. I've gotten so used to Jaeger carrying me that I barely notice the stares.

"Wait," I ask as we enter the musty basement, passing more groups of chatting people to enter a long, low-ceilinged room filled with folding chairs. "Who is Father Francis?"

"A priest at St. Xavier's downtown. He founded Hierony-mus' School for the Lost."

I've heard of St. Xavier's. It's a medieval-looking church on the edge of midtown. Now that I think of it, I've heard of the school. It's an orphanage.

"You and Kaiser went to St. Xavier's?"

Jaeger finds us seats on the edge of the room. Most people have congregated by the entrance or the table in the back that holds boxes of day-old sugar donuts and a coffee urn that dispenses black tar.

He's positioned me so he's between me and the door. He's also constantly sweeping the place. He keeps a hand on my thigh, and I feel lucky he didn't make me sit on his lap.

"Yes and no. We attended mass only on the coldest days. Father Francis founded a soup kitchen, and we started to bring in street kids, the ones too young to fend for themselves. That's when the Father founded the school and raised the money to build the dormitories."

I stare at him. I've sensed his upbringing was rough, but I had no idea it was this bad. "How old were you?"

He shrugs. "Nine or ten."

I suck in a breath. *So young.* "Did you stay at the school?"

"A night or two. Kaiser and I were too wild to stay put. But Hieronymus is where we met the Devil and St. James. They're the ones who ended up founding Fraternitas."

There are tons of rumors and speculation swirling around the brotherhood and the man called the Devil. Honey would be delighted that I could give her answers.

I don't care about Fraternitas. I want to ask more questions about Jaeger and Kaiser, two school-age kids without a home.

But the meeting is about to start. More people flood the room.

"Hey, Elodie." One of the meeting attendees shuffles closer, donut in hand. I recognize his blue hair and thin face.

"Hey, Tommy."

"Hiya." He raises a hand to greet Jaeger. Jaeger just looks at him.

"Tommy, this is Jaeger," I say quickly. "A... friend."

Jaeger cups my hand with both of his.

"More than a friend," I amend.

Tommy's eyes flash down to the ring on my hand and then Jaeger's skull ring. "Uh, got it. See ya." He backs away, beating it for a seat by the door.

I sigh. "Please don't intimidate people here." I met Tommy in my early NA days. He and I have exchanged numbers so we could support each other through the twelve steps.

"I won't." Jaeger dips his head so only I can hear. "Just any friends who are more than friends."

"There isn't anyone like that here." I check to see if

Tommy's okay, and he's chatting with someone else while eating his donut. I transfer my glare to Jaeger. "Besides you. You know this."

He sits back, looking satisfied, but keeps my hand between both of his.

Today's meeting has a speaker, so after we welcome newcomers and recite the Serenity Prayer, a woman with box braids stands and shares her story.

The church basement is both cold and drafty and clammy, with the heat of all the bodies crowded together, and it smells like sweat and stale smoke.

I let the speaker's story wash over me, crying a little at the sad parts like I would at a movie. Her story has a happy ending, though, because she's here and sharing. For a lot of people in this room, the story won't end well, but that's life. We all live a million stories, and whether the theme is horrific or heroic depends on which moments you choose to showcase.

Jaeger's hands are warm on mine. In this crowd, he stands out, not just because he's bigger than anyone else. He has a sort of glow, like a saint in a classical painting. Maybe it's his handsome face or golden hair. Or his air of calm command. He looks more real than everyone else, spotlit so the rest of the room fades away.

At one point, he gets up and leaves my side. I miss his heat and am glad when he returns with a box of tissues for me. He takes one and wipes my tears away.

"Thank you," I mouth to him. He cups my face a moment, gazing at me with such intensity that I look away. But I wonder what he's thinking. Is he judging all of us addicts here? I've never brought a guy here. I haven't dated anyone since getting clean. And I never would've imagined someone like Jaeger being at my side. Is he okay with being here?

Will he see me differently now that he knows I'm an addict?

The meeting ends. The mood is lighter, as if the speaker's story was all our stories, and our collective confession allows us to leave some shadows behind.

Jaeger intuits that I don't want to stick around or talk to anyone. He picks me up, ignoring the raised eyebrows. I wave to Tommy when we pass him, and he waves back. I'll text him later and tell him it was good to see him.

Outside, a light rain greets us. The Lykan is still at the curb. A cop car is live, parked close by, but there's no ticket on the hood.

We sit in the car for a moment, watching the drops of water slide down the windshield.

"You should know I haven't used in three years," I say. "I went through a hard time when I had to drop out of school."

Jaeger squeezes my hand and doesn't speak. His silence makes it easier to tell him the rest.

"My boyfriend at the time... liked to party. I went through... some stuff. In college. And I thought that partying would help." I have few memories of those nights—nothing but flashing lights, dirty floors of clubs, and the sandy feeling in my eyes and mouth. Daylight was like knives in my skull, and I was tired all the time, bone-deep exhaustion I'd felt like I was too young to feel. "We broke up when I decided to stop using. Margot was pregnant and not doing well, and I knew I had to help. The pills were an escape I couldn't afford."

He turns in the seat, facing me. He cups my cheek and says nothing. I lean into his palm.

"Life is hard," I say. "But other people have it worse."

He strokes his thumb over my lips. "Was it hard working at Inferno?"

"Do you mean was there temptation? There's always temptation. But I've learned..." I try to put my thoughts into words. "This... this moment is real. Even if it hurts, it's worth the pain. The high was fake. And it didn't last."

He nods, and my heart beats faster with the feeling that he understands. "And there are other pleasures," he says.

"Yes."

"Like this." He leans in and brushes his lips over mine. I crane my neck to get closer, wanting more.

"You are so beautiful," he murmurs against my mouth. "So brave."

The warmth in his voice is a deep pool I want to sink into. I want to hold him, to mold my body to his, to be so close to him that his warmth sinks into me and heals all my broken parts. I've spent so many years trying to hold myself together, and now here's this man willing to wrap his strong arms around me and make a safe space for me so I can rest.

I would unbuckle my seatbelt and climb into his lap, but there's a cop right there, so I say, "Take me home."

He puts the Lykan in gear.

I stare at him the whole drive, memorizing the way the light and shadow slide over his features.

I don't think twice about the fact that I called his penthouse 'home.'

~

JAEGER

. . .

I LIE IN BED, Elodie drowsing in my arms. She's naked, her short legs tangled with mine. I can't stop running my hands over her soft skin. She has the sweetest freckles on her shoulders, and her plush thighs are dimpled and silky to the touch.

Her ankle is looking better. These past few days, she's been able to rest and heal. I leave her as little as possible, but when duty calls, I know she's safe and warm. I come home to her curled up on the couch under several layers of fluffy blankets, watching home renovation shows. A cozy bunny in her den.

She's right where I want her. When she's like this, comfortable and freshly fucked, she forgets to fight me, forgets herself, and relaxes into the moment. She's content.

But I fear when she's healed, she'll decide it's best for her to leave. I have to find new ways to trap her, to draw her down into my world.

There are several ways I could do this. I splay my hand over her plush belly. She's gloriously round and soft now. What will she look like when I fill her with my baby? Atticus could easily sedate her and give her a fertility shot. I file that away as a later option. There might be an easier way.

In recent days, she's opened up to me, telling me about her past. She thought she would scare me off. She doesn't know me if she thinks I'll scare easily. I would kill for her. Going to a meeting and supporting her recovery is the least I can do.

But she still fears my lifestyle. My brothers. Fraternitas. I must show her there's a place for her. In my bed, as my woman. At my side, spoiled as my sweet pet. Kneeling at my feet, wearing my collar.

I will introduce her to my brothers and fight for them to accept her. And then I will teach her where she belongs.

ELODIE

"I HAVE AN ERRAND," Jaeger tells me.

I've been sitting on the couch, scrolling social media on my phone with rom-coms playing in the background. I think about reaching out to friends from school, but it feels like my old life. When I read a few of their posts gushing over "Professor Roylin's brilliant lecture," my stomach got tight, and I deleted the app.

So when Jaeger insists I accompany him on this errand, I'm glad to get out of the penthouse.

He drives through the city, weaving through the high rises of midtown until the grand spires of a cathedral appear. St. Xavier's. I recognize the shining, white stone and the grand church steps.

I expect Jaeger to illegally park right in front of it like he always does, but he turns into a small side parking lot with a wheelchair ramp entrance.

As Jaeger carries me in, the bells in the tower begin to toll. The place is hushed and smells clean, with a faint whiff of smoke and spices from the incense. He heads deep into the church, crossing a checkered marble floor and a line of white columns to enter the cavernous sanctuary.

My mouth falls open at the soaring high ceilings and gothic windows. I wasn't raised Catholic, so I have no idea what scenes are depicted in the jewel-toned stained glass, but small golden plaques underneath announce the "Stations of the Cross." In between the windows are a series of stone alcoves, each one with a different white marble statue. The place is opulent, far more than I realized. Maybe a lot of wealthy people attend church here, and the parish uses their donations to decorate, as well as run the school and orphanage.

There's no one here now. I haven't seen a hint of a single person. The quiet has a weight to it, and I clamp my lips shut, unwilling to disturb the sacred silence.

Jaeger strides confidently down the center aisle and sets me down in a polished pew. "Wait here."

What? He walks past the altar and disappears into a small back door beyond the choir stands.

I sit uncomfortably, bathed in yellow and red light from one of the stained glass windows. In the quiet, I can hear the shrieks of children playing outside. It would make sense that the children's home has a playground nearby.

What did Jaeger tell me? *We attended mass only on the coldest days.* I try to imagine him and his brother lurking in the back of this beautiful room, their skin chapped red from the cold. *Father Francis founded the school. We brought street kids, the ones too young to fend for themselves. . .*

"Can I help you?"

I jolt in my seat at the unexpected voice. A man stands in the aisle next to me. I didn't hear him approach.

"Pardon me. I didn't mean to startle you." He puts out a hand and hovers it near my shoulder in a reassuring gesture, although he doesn't touch me. He's white, with thick, light brown hair and a short beard. He's in his mid to late forties, with a weathered face.

He's in black robes with a white collar and a large wooden cross on a chain around his neck. A priest.

"Um... I'm okay. I'm here with a friend. He said he had an errand." I wave toward the front of the church where Jaeger went. "If I'm not supposed to be here, I can leave..."

"No, not at all. The church is open at all hours to anyone

who wishes to worship." He relaxes back against one of the pews, studying me.

I tense further. "Oh, I'm not here to... do that. I'm not religious."

"I know why you're here, Elodie."

A chill runs through me. How does he know my name?

He chuckles. "I suspect Jaeger brought you here so we could meet." His blue eyes crinkle with laugh lines, but something about his gaze is unnerving. "I'm Father Francis."

10

E *lodie*

I STARE up at the man Jaeger told me about.

"But..." Jaeger said Father Francis raised him. This man doesn't look old enough to have raised a grown man. "I didn't realize," I finish.

Father Francis doesn't seem ruffled by my scrutiny of him.

"I've known Jaeger a long time," he says, as if he can hear my thoughts. "Since he was a boy. I took my position here when I was twenty-six. At the time, this was a poor parish with an aging clergy and a church building in need of renovation. No one wanted a position here." He glances around the gorgeous sanctuary.

I find my voice and follow his gaze to take in the finery surrounding us. "This place is beautiful."

"We're blessed now with some very generous donors. I

believe you've met a few of them by working at Inferno." Father Francis folds his hands in front of him, looking at me expectantly as if he's said something revealing.

Is this place connected to Fraternitas? Jaeger said he and St. James were raised by Father Francis, along with the head of the organization, a man I only know as The Devil.

Could the brotherhood be the church's main donor? It would make sense if they wanted to give back to the man who'd helped them and so many other kids.

Does a priest really associate with a gang leader called The Devil?

"Maybe," I say. I glance at his hands, checking for a skull ring.

With a sly smile, he raises his hands and shows me the front and back. His fingers are bare. The only jewelry he's wearing is the cross.

Instead of feeling relieved, I tense up further. He seems to be reading my mind. And is amused by my scrutiny.

He's a priest, for godssakes. So why do I feel like a shark is circling me in the water?

"I know you've met St. James," he says.

Ah yes. Anyone associated with St. James isn't someone I'll let my guard down around. Although it's ironic how much a soulless man like St. James is involved with a church.

"Why do you think Jaeger wanted us to meet?" I ask.

He cocks his head. "You don't know?" He presses his lips together, and I get the feeling that while I had once been an interesting specimen, now I've disappointed him. "I suppose it's not for me to explain."

What the fuck does that mean? I open my mouth to ask, but he continues, "Suffice it to say, Jaeger is very important to me. And he knows I'd want to meet anyone important to him."

My rude retort dies on my tongue.

Father Francis's eyes narrow at my speechlessness. Before he can say anymore, I hear my name.

"Elodie." Jaeger appears, walking back from the altar. He comes to me and slides me into his arms before facing Father Francis. "I see you've met each other."

"Yes," Father Francis says. "We were just speaking of you."

"Nothing bad, I hope." Jaeger smiles but searches my face. I must look a little shell-shocked.

I feel like I've been called to meet Jaeger's one and only parent without any warning.

I guess I have.

A shadow slants across us as another figure winds around the altar. It's Kaiser, dressed in jeans and a leather jacket, black from head to toe. He glares at us. Without a word of greeting, he makes his way down the side aisle and leaves.

I look from Kaiser's retreating back to Jaeger. Were the brothers meeting here? Or did Kaiser just happen to be here?

What is going on?

Jaeger returns my gaze but says nothing.

"It's lovely to see you here, Jaeger," Father Francis says. "Will you two stay for mass?"

Jaeger shakes his head.

"Ah, well,"—the priest shrugs—"I had to ask."

"*Dum spiro spero*," Jaeger says, and Father Francis grins.

"I see some of the Latin lessons stuck." Father Francis stands to let Jaeger pass. "Goodbye, then. And good to meet you, Elodie. I have a feeling we'll be seeing more of each other." He stands in the aisle and watches us exit.

"What did you say?" I ask Jaeger as he carries me away.

"It's Latin. 'While I breathe, I hope.'"

He carries me out, and at the top of the steps, I can see into the next lot, which has a playground filled with children.

"Is that the school?" I point to it.

"Yes."

I crane my head as we pass the fence, but I can't see more than a modest brick building five or six stories high with many windows.

Jaeger told me he hadn't attended the school, but obviously, Father Francis tried to give him an education anyway. It makes sense. Some of Jaeger's manners and way of speaking are oddly formal. And I've never met a thug who knows Latin.

He sets me in the car and heads around to the driver's side. He still hasn't told me what he was doing or why Kaiser was there.

"Did you get your errand done?" I probe.

"Yes." He puts his hand on the stick shift but pauses, turning to give me a long look.

I want to ask him more about his brother and Father Francis and what errand required him to visit the church, but I don't. I lick my lips and settle back in the seat. Jaeger puts the car in gear, and we leave St. Xavier's and Father Francis behind.

~

"ELODIE," a deep voice calls my name. "Elodie, wake up."

I come awake with a gasp. I'm in the dark bedroom with

Jaeger beside me. He's propped up on an elbow, his free hand on my shoulder. He orders the lights to turn on the lowest level.

"You were having a bad dream."

I'm still in its clutches. There was a dark tunnel of trees, and I was running like I did with Jaeger. But it wasn't him chasing me. It was someone from the past, someone I've tried hard to forget.

I'm covered in a cold sweat, gripping the blankets. I suck in a breath to come back into myself.

Jaeger tucks a curl behind my ear. "You okay?"

"I'm fine."

"You want to tell me about it?"

Instead of answering, I curl toward him, tucking my face into his chest. We've grown closer these past few days, but I don't want to tell him about that part of my past. It'll bring up too many questions. He'll find out the most traumatic thing that ever happened to me.

Jaeger isn't the worst predator I've ever met. He's bigger and badder and way more dangerous, but obviously, my psyche thinks he's safe. That's why I'm dreaming about the past—so I can purge it. Deep down, I know if I tell him the story about the man who hurt me, Jaeger would make sure that man paid the price for what he did.

Jaeger wraps his arms around me and kisses the top of my head. I'm relaxed and starting to drift back to sleep when he slips his hand between my legs.

I open my eyes, coming awake. The lights are still on, low enough for me to fall asleep but bright enough for me to see the gleam in Jaeger's stormy eyes. It has to be around midnight, and he's already fucked me, so I'm not sure what's going on. Maybe he wants me to forget my nightmare?

For a moment, he only strokes me, holding my gaze as

his thumb tickles my clit. My hips start to move, and he stops until I grow still, and then he starts stroking me again.

"I'll be gone most of the day tomorrow. Will you miss me?"

I stare at him. He's trying to have a conversation, now?

He stops touching me. "Will you miss me?"

Yes. My body knows the right answer. "No," I lie. Each day has me closer to healing fully and escaping.

Except I haven't thought much of escaping lately. Yeah, I'm weirded out by all the Fraternitas stuff and today's outing to meet Father Frances. But I'm loving my lazy days in this gorgeous penthouse. Going on the run will mean living out of gross, pay-by-the-day motels, places that take cash so I can fly under the radar. I'll have to find a place to hide out. Get a new job.

It'll suck, but that's life. We're all running and running until death catches us.

With enough running, I might be able to forget Jaeger, who's currently frowning at me like he can read my thoughts. I wipe my face clear of expression.

"What?"

"Hmmm." He goes back to stroking me, running his thumb up and down the seam of my lower lips. I want to grab his wrist and grind against his hand, but I don't want to break the spell. My orgasm creeps closer as the seconds tick by. I'm about to ride the gentle swell, but he pauses again.

"What did you think of my brother?" he asks, and my pleasure dies, remembering Jaeger's face on a cold-eyed stranger. It was a shock to see him at St. Xavier's.

"I don't think he likes me. Like, at all." I shudder, remembering his threats outside the women's bathroom at Inferno.

Jaeger dismisses this with a toss of his head. "He doesn't like anyone."

"Not even you?" I got the feeling Kaiser threatened me out of a protective instinct for his brother.

Jaeger takes my hand and transfers it to the bulging pectoral muscle under his collarbone. My fingers graze the raised ridge of a long-healed wound. I've come to realize his tattoos hide a maze of scars. This one is large and very close to his heart.

"What's this?"

"From the time Kaiser tried to kill me."

My fingers freeze on his chest. "What? Why?"

"It was when we were young. Do not worry. He probably won't ever do it again."

I'm speechless, and my body's gone cold. Jaeger shifts under me, and my leg brushes his hard cock. A minute ago, I would've rolled onto my back to receive him, but now I'm fighting the urge to curl into a ball.

Is he telling me this because he wants me to share about my own nightmares?

The scar is so real under my fingertips. I shouldn't pry into Jaeger's violent past. I've kept my head in the sand this long. And yet...

"How old were you?" I ask.

He smiles. "Fifteen."

I suck in a breath.

"We were in the fighting rings. The ones under the city."

"The ones Fraternitas runs?"

"At the time, Fraternitas did not run them because Fraternitas barely existed. Kaiser and I were under the care"—another bleak smile—"of a man named Maestro. He was our guardian in name. He stole us off the streets and kept us captive. And when we were of age, he made us fight."

My breath is frozen in my lungs. Terrible images flood

my mind. My veins feel tight like they used to when I was craving a hit.

"What age?" I whisper.

"He took ownership of us after we hit puberty. We spent a year and a half in the rings."

I run my hands over his shoulders and chest, finding the bumps and ragged edges of his scars under the ink. I knew his life had been brutal. I didn't realize the violence had started when he was so young.

"What about Father Francis?"

"He searched for us. So did St. James and all the rest of the street children who would become Fraternitas. Maestro hid Kaiser and me away in a place where they could not find us. Until the day we broke free."

My fingers find the scar over his heart. "What happened?"

"We killed him. After he made us fight each other, and Kaiser gave me this." He covers my hand with his large one, molding my palm to his marred chest. Our hands rise and fall with his breath. "To save my life. To save both our lives. Maestro decreed that one of us would fall, and so I did. And as I lay bleeding out, Kaiser turned on Maestro and killed him."

I close my eyes, but the scene Jaeger described plays out in my mind. Over and over, unending. Two identical blond-haired boys, wild and covered in blood, grappling in a shadowy circle.

Jaeger rubs the top of my hand, and my eyes snap open. I stare into the stormy seas of his irises, feeling like I've seen every part of him, inside and out. I've never been so close to anyone.

I've never let someone get so close to me. Our breath mingles and becomes one. "Why are you telling me this?"

"I know you want me, Elodie. But you're also afraid."

I roll away from him and curl into a ball. He rolls, too, surrounding me. His hard dick prods my backside, but he keeps his hand threaded with mine, clasped against my heart.

His lips find my ear. "Did you know the night we met was my birthday? You were St. James' gift to me." His tone is soft with wonder. "I've never had a birthday gift before. Maestro kept us in cages."

I squeeze my eyes tighter.

He continues so softly I can't be sure I haven't imagined it. "I know you don't want to know this about me. I know you want to run." His breath stirs the curls at the back of my neck. "But you're brave, braver than you know." He's so close his lips brush the back of my ear. "I've never told anyone these things, Elodie. Not even Father Francis or my Fraternitas brothers. Kaiser and I never speak of it. But if there's a chance someone in this world will know everything about me, I want it to be you."

11

E lodie

THE NEXT MORNING, Jaeger wakes me with his face between my legs. I come awake, my arousal shooting from zero to a million miles per hour. My body is primed from his late-night touching, and all the heaviness of last night's confession and my intense dreams disappear.

I writhe, fighting his grip on my thighs as he eats me like he's starving, and I'm the best thing he's ever tasted. My climax spirals closer, coming within reach. My pussy squeezes around his single finger. I just need a little more—

He stops and sits up. My inner muscles clench on nothing, begging for stimulation.

"Wha—?" I stare at him. "What are you doing?"

"Making sure you miss me." Jaeger rubs my belly. I wait for his hand to slide between my legs, but it doesn't move any further. "Do you need the bathroom?"

I need to orgasm! But I nod. He carries me to the bathroom and lets me do my business.

When we get back to the bed, he leans in to kiss me. I slide a hand under the silky fall of his hair, cupping the back of his neck to keep him close.

He pushes forward, forcing me to lie back on the bed. His hands roam over my body, his lips never leaving mine.

This is more like it. His big body covers mine, and my core is heating up, ready for him to spread my legs and dominate me.

I'm shuddering under him when he breaks the kiss.

"Ah, ah." He wags a finger.

"Jaeger—" My mouth falls open when he leaves the bed and walks naked to the closet, leaving me bereft.

What is he up to? I remember our conversation last night. All the intense things he told me in the pocket of midnight. His teenage years, the trauma, the scars. He said he wants to know me. Last night proves he wants me to know him, too.

And now I know enough to imagine as a little boy, growing up with no one to take care of him. How does he know how to take care of me so well?

He deserves someone to take care of him. And I feel all warm and hopeful, imagining that that someone is me.

But it's overwhelming, too. He's only been in my life a short time. It's been so much, so fast, and I'm afraid of how much I'm leaning on him.

I don't know what to do with any of it.

I can't think over the ache in my core.

He thinks he can tease me and leave me? I can take care of myself.

I sink into the pillows and slide my hand between my legs. My own fingers are small and dainty compared to

Jaeger's rough digits. I use my free hand to pinch my nipples. The spark of pain gets me closer to the edge.

"Ah, ah." Jaeger leans over more, grabbing my wrists. He straddles me—yay!—but instead of sinking into my wet folds and punishing me with hard thrusts of his cock, he pins my arms over my head and fiddles with something on the headboard.

Then he moves off me. I go to move my arms, but they remain overhead. "What the—" I crane my head. He buckled cuffs around my wrists, leaving them chained to the headboard. I try to reach my right hand to my left to see if I can undo the cuffs, but the chain is just short enough that one hand can't reach the other.

"Jaeger?" I wrack the chains, making them snap against the wood. "What is this?"

He sets a hand on my thigh. "No touching." He leans in to kiss me. I growl and turn my head, and his stubble prickles against my cheek instead.

He rises and pulls on his shirt, completing his usual uniform of jeans and a T-shirt. Meanwhile, I'm naked, trying to pull myself up to see if I can loosen the leather tongue of the buckle with my teeth.

"No." He returns, grabs my left ankle, and pulls me back down. I try to kick him, but he holds me easily while he fishes at the foot of the bed for more restraints. I end up with my left ankle cuffed and the rest of my body immobilized with a strap around my midsection.

"There." He places a pillow under my right ankle, elevating it. I twist, but I can't move far.

I'm panting when he walks around the bed, checking each of my bindings and testing the circulation in my fingers. My outrage made my orgasm die, but something about his proximity, his scent, and the fact that I'm tied down scrambles my mind. My pussy throbs with need.

"Why are you doing this?" I ask to keep from begging him to touch me.

"I'm making sure you can't touch yourself." He swipes his fingers between my legs, grazing my folds and making my thighs quiver. He licks my taste off while he holds my gaze. I flush but grow panicked when he turns away.

"Jaeger." I tug the bindings. "I need you."

"I know." He stalls in the doorway. "I'll be back."

"Where are you going?" I wrestle with the cuffs in earnest, but they hold fast. "Don't leave me."

"Don't worry, bunny." He shows me his phone. On it is an image of me as I am now, in bed. He points to the ceiling in the corner of the room. "I have a camera. I'll monitor you the whole time."

Un-fucking-believable! "Jaeger, if you leave, so help me—"

"Bye, bunny." He closes the door.

I sag back onto the bed. That bastard!

I wait for him to return, but the minutes drag by. There's no clock in his room, so I can only guess the time by how the brightening light under the crack of the door shows the sun getting higher in the sky.

I spend a while trying to wriggle into a position that will let me reach the cuffs, but it's no use. I end up sweaty with my arms and left thigh sore from straining against the chains.

A million years later, the door creaks open, and Jaeger appears holding a black cloth bag.

"Still here, bunny?" he chuckles. "Of course you are." He sits down and holds a bottle of water to my lips.

I glare at him but drink up. He gives me the full bottle

and then feeds me a smoothie with a straw. He unties me long enough to go to the bathroom but then carries me back to bed and ties me up again.

"Are you going to leave me like this again?"

"Yes. Still hungry?"

I shake my head.

"You're being so good for me." He reaches into the black bag and pulls out a pink dildo affixed to a set of black leather straps. "Let's see if we can make this more interesting."

"Jaeger, please—" I struggle, but I can't stop him from pinning me and slipping the dildo inside me. I'm so wet it glides right in, and I moan at how it fills me. It's nice, but not enough to let me orgasm. He finishes buckling the small straps around the tops of my thighs and securing the harness that keeps the dildo inside me.

"This isn't fair," I whine.

"I know. That's why it's fun." He drops a kiss on my nose. I bare my teeth at him.

The vibrator buzzes to life. My growl turns into a yelp. I come off the bed as much as the bondage will allow. The toy presses against all the delicious spots inside me, teasing me until I'm panting. Every muscle in me clenches, but as I get close to orgasm, the vibrator dies.

I sag into the bed, too overcome to speak.

"I'll be back, bunny," he says, and he leaves. I struggle to escape but get nowhere before the vibrator surges inside me again.

I don't know how long he leaves me like this. All I know is the intense moments when the vibrator is on and torturing me. I squeeze my thighs together, clenching around it, but I can't get the right angle to trigger my climax. Sweat trickles down my temple. My inner muscles scream when I tense them. All too soon, the vibrator dies. I bite back a scream and count down the seconds before it starts up again.

When he walks in, many vibrator rounds later, I am one hundred percent a cranky bunny. It doesn't help that he looks just as hot as when he left, not one golden hair out of place.

"You," I growl.

"Me." He settles on the bed but makes no move to free me.

"You left me. All day." I rack the chains to emphasize my words.

"You want something, bunny?" He brushes his fingers over my breast, and I fight the urge to arch into his touch.

"You know what I want."

"Mmm." He squeezes my breast, and I sigh. His mouth descends. His tongue flicks my nipple.

I fist my fingers in the pillowcase. I want him to fuck me. I want him to untie me so I can slap him and force his face between my legs.

It's frightening how much I need him.

He raises his head, a wicked gleam in his stormy eyes. "A little longer, I think."

"No!"

But he doesn't listen. He fits an attachment to the dildo, one that slips between my ass cheeks and stimulates my sensitive entrance back there. I squirm but can't dislodge it. It adds another delicious dimension to my arousal. Delicious and disturbing. I never knew how good a vibrator there would feel.

This time, he leaves me for longer. Time has no meaning. The light under the door deepens to amber and disappears, chased by shadows.

By the time the door creaks open again, I'm relieved to see him but too exhausted to move. My skin glistens from my straining.

He removes the toy, and I'm not even embarrassed at the wet squelch it makes when it leaves my pussy. He undoes the bindings around my waist and leg, and I whimper.

"Jaeger, you have to help me."

"I will, bunny. Shhh." He pulls me into his arms and kisses me. He frees me from the chains so he can lift me off the bed but keeps the cuffs around my wrists. He clips them together so my hands are still bound.

"No touching," he warns. I'm so wrung out that I nod. Anything to be free of the low-grade torture.

He takes me to the bathroom and then rinses me in the shower. I sit and let him wash me. He's careful with the sprayer around my swollen pussy. I spread my legs wide, and he shakes his head.

He's not going to let me cum. But the fact that he's denying me is extra hot. It disturbs me how much it turns me on.

I have the feeling he's preparing me for something, but I don't want to ask what. I'm afraid I already know.

After a dinner that he hand-feeds me, I'm feeling more myself. He clips my cuffs to the side of the chair and leaves me for a moment before returning and carrying me to the bed, where he's changed the sheets.

"I'm going to uncuff you, but if I catch you touching yourself, you will remain tied up all night and all tomorrow."

"Fine." I offer him my wrists. He removes the cuffs and rubs the red marks, even kissing them. The brush of his lips sends flutters through my belly.

Which reminds me... "What happens if I cum accidentally?"

"You will be punished." The look he gives me sears both fear and excitement into me. "And you will not like it."

I wish I were brave enough to do it anyway. What sort of punishment are we talking about here?

It's as though he can read my mind. "There are metal chastity belts made to be worn all day. They cover everything, from here to here." He hovers a hand over my pussy, then runs a hand over my ass. "You think one day is hard? Try a whole week."

My head goes back a beat. "You wouldn't."

"I would." He's dead-eyed, scarily serious, enough that I shrink from him.

"But"—I glance at the front of his jeans, which are tented with his erection—"you're not cumming either."

"It'll be worth it." He kisses my forehead. Just the touch of his lips gives me lower belly flutters. I want to cry. He draws back and sees my expression. "Don't pout." He tucks me into the blankets, making sure my hands are on top of the covers.

How am I going to sleep with this throbbing in my pussy?

Jaeger strips off his jeans, and his dick is like a flagpole. I'd salute it if I were in a better mood.

I look at it sadly until he covers himself with a blanket.

"I hate you," I tell him.

He grins and runs a thumb over my lips. I tilt my head back, my breath growing heavy.

He takes his hand away, and I growl deep in my throat. I didn't realize I made growling noises all the time until he pointed it out. "I am going to kill you." He's definitely higher on my People I'd Like to Kill list.

"Talk to me; take your mind off it."

Oh, now he wants to talk? I remember how deep things got last night and shake my head. "No."

He stretches out next to me like we're having a lazy post-coital chat. It sucks because his presence, scent, and heat are triggers for my arousal now. My clit is throbbing so hard I want to scream.

"You never told me what you think of my brother," he says.

"He's on the list," I mutter.

"What list?"

"The list of people I want to kill," I say because my filter is gone.

He looks amused. "Am I at the top of the list?"

I roll my eyes. Mr. Ego. "No." Although, he might be if he doesn't let me cum soon.

He cocks his head to the side. "Then who is?"

"Why does it matter? Aren't you upset that you're on the list?"

He shrugs. "I am on many such lists. You're the first person to tell me outright." He grins like this pleases him. "Now tell me. Who else do you want to kill?"

I wriggle to my side, turning away so it's clear I'm ending this conversation.

He rolls me over. "I have ways of making you talk."

"What are you going to do? Sprain my other ankle?"

He cups my breast, grazing my nipple with his thumb. "No. Not when there are more fun things I could do to you."

I push his hand away, but he simply lets it fall to my waist.

"You know what I do for Fraternitas?"

"You work for them." I've tried not to think about this too much, but it's easy to put the pieces together. And after last night's confessional, I feel like we've trespassed miles beyond the boundary I'd set if I were smart. "Like an enforcer?" I guess.

"That's one word for it. I am the muscle. Fraternitas' show of strength. I take out the trash." So, the murders he committed in the stairwell weren't his first. His job is to kill people or make them disappear.

His ringed hand rests on my hip. A killer's hand, big enough to squeeze the life out of a victim, his face the last thing they see.

But it's such a nice face. I reach up and touch it because I can. No one else gets to see him like this, touch him like this.

It makes me feel powerful.

His cheek curls into my palm. His stubble scrapes my palm. "You pretend to be mean and hateful, but deep down, you're sweet."

"No, I'm not." I shift in the sheets, trying to get my surging arousal to calm down. "Shut up. I'm a psycho killer like you."

His voice is warm like it gets when he's cooing sweet nothings in my ear after sex. "Bunny—"

"I'm an attack rabbit of death." I place a finger on his lips. "I'm warning you."

He licks my finger and then swallows it. I close my eyes, dizzy with desire.

"Gods, Jaeger…"

He pulls my finger out of his mouth and kisses the tip. "I want to know who you want to kill."

"No one." I go to roll away again, and he stops me. We end up wrestling, which leaves me pinned under him, breathing hard and ready for a good hard fuck.

I tilt my hips. "If I tell you, will you fuck me?"

"I will… later."

I squint at him. "How much later?"

"At a time and place of my choosing."

All this edging has a purpose, then. He has plans for me. "Then no." I'll torture him like he's torturing me.

"I'll touch you—"

I grab his hand before he can touch my pussy to edge me further. "Nope. I'm a nun." He looks delighted by this, and I'm in a goofy state from all the edging and denial, so I continue. "No more kill list for me. I'm taking a vow of non-violence. I have forgiveness in my heart."

He's smiling when he reaches down and smacks the side of my ass. "Liar." But he doesn't press me. He sinks back down to the bed, tucking me against him. He calls for the bedroom lights to blink off.

In the dark womb of the room, there's only the sound of our breathing. My longing for him dies to a simmer that's less painful but no less potent. We're back in the late-night sanctuary where everything is peaceful, even my racing thoughts.

"I want to kill so many people," I admit to the darkness. "So many. But you wouldn't understand."

His hand comes to rest on my throat. "Tell me."

We're not joking anymore. But he's shared so much with me that I feel like he's earned my secrets.

"You don't know what it's like." The words burn like acid in my throat. "You're bigger and stronger than anyone. People don't mess with you. Half of them look like they want to run away when you walk into a room. It's not like that for me. Everyone shits on me. The creepy landlord, my boss, even you." I'm clenching my fists. "And I just have to take it." My teeth ache from clenching them, so I loosen my jaw and draw a shuddering breath. "So I made a list, and I imagine what it would be like to be strong."

Jaeger and Kaiser aren't at the top of the list. Not even close. At the top are the dirtbags who wrecked me, who took without giving back, who let me love them and then left like I didn't matter. And the worst man of all is the one who took advantage of his position over me and destroyed my life and my peace to the point where I had to drop out of school.

I'm not ready to tell Jaeger about them, and he doesn't press.

"I'm sorry, bunny."

"For what?" I let out a bitter laugh. "That's life. The strong crush the weak. Some people are predators. The rest of us are prey. All we can do is try to survive."

He rubs my back. It's soothing, but I know he bears a ring on his finger that marks him as a predator.

"I wasn't always bigger than everyone," he says. "On the streets, I was prey."

I don't have anything to say to that because he told me the barest details about his enslavement to the man called Maestro, and they were so horrible I can't wrap my head around them.

"I didn't want to live like that anymore. Neither did my brothers. And so we became Fraternitas."

I understand that. If I'd lived through what he's lived through, I'd do anything to become powerful, too. You become the predator, or you die as prey.

Like I said, in the end, we're all just trying to survive.

I grab his hand and squeeze it. "I'm sorry, too." In this midnight confessional, we are each other's witnesses.

But absolution is something we can only give ourselves.

12

E *lodie*

I DREAM of touching myself but wake up whimpering, Jaeger stroking the tops of my thighs. My skin is coated with my dripping essence. "Jaeger, please." I shudder, needing release. "Please let me..."

"Later." He kisses my cheek. "Not yet."

I groan but don't make a move to touch myself when he pulls away.

"I have to go somewhere again today. If I don't tie you up, will you be a good girl?"

I nod vigorously. Anything to escape another long day straining against the vibrator.

He narrows his eyes, but whatever he sees in me convinces him I'm telling the truth. "You're being so good for me, bunny." He nuzzles my cheek, and I turn my head away. The feel of his stubble against my skin is too much.

I don't know what he's planning, but he's up to something, and I'm afraid to know. Whatever it is, it's big.

He pulls away, and we go through our morning routine. He helps me dress in wide-leg jeans and a fitted white top.

It's not until he's set me on the couch with my ankle propped up that he tells me, "I invited your friends to visit."

"Friends? What friends?"

He leans down to light the cluster of candles on the coffee table and straightens. "The girls from Inferno."

"Honey and Daria? You invited them? You're letting them come here?"

"It's your home, too."

I press my lips together. Sure, I'm living here, but it's not really my place.

"They'll be here soon. I ordered food. The doorman will let them in."

I clutch a cashmere throw to my chest, watching him move around the room, making the place as cozy as the rom-com set of my dreams.

He answers the door for the food delivery and kisses me before he leaves. "Remember, no touching. Or there'll be consequences."

My friends arrive in time for a late brunch. We've never hung out outside of work like this, so I'm nervous about how it will go. At least Jaeger's penthouse will be a nicer place to hang out than my old apartment.

Daria enters slowly, craning her head to look all around. She greets me with a nod, keeping her hands stuffed into her black leather jacket.

The next to enter is Angel, one of the dancers at Inferno. "Hey, girl," she grins at me. "Okay if I crash this party?"

"Of course," I say. I don't know Angel very well, but she

seems sweet. On stage, she mostly wears wigs, but her hair is long, straight, and dyed black.

Honey bounces in, all smiles in a taupe bodycon dress, with her hair in ringlet curls. "Elodie! You look amazing! Who did your hair?"

"Hey, Honey. You look great, too." I don't tell her Jaeger did my hair. He doesn't look like he's capable of it, but he's better at doing my hair than I ever was. He seems to enjoy taking the time to pamper me. The shelf in the shower is filled with hair masks and special conditioners for my curls, and the results have been fabulous. My skin glows, and my shining curls are behaving better than I've been able to achieve.

Honey's already moved on. "Omigosh," she cries when she sees the brunch spread Jaeger ordered. Angel joins her, grabbing a strawberry from a bowl of cut fruit.

"So this is his place, huh?" Daria lingers in the entryway, leaning to look through the open door to our bedroom.

"This is it," I wave her in. "Feel free to snoop."

Honey laughs, and Daria's shoulders drift down an inch.

"C'mon," Angel beckons. Her plate is already filled with bacon and pancakes. The food tempts Daria enough to join the other two.

"You look good," Honey says.

"Thanks." I accept her offer for more coffee and caramel creamer.

"Girl, this place..." Angel says.

"I know," I say.

Daria's still in the kitchen area, opening cabinets and checking them out. I wouldn't be surprised if she figured out the location of Jaeger's safe.

"I like it," Honey announces. Angel gives her a fond look, and Daria rolls her eyes. It's obvious any member of Fraternitas has Honey's stamp of approval. I worry about her lack of self-preservation.

"Has he said anything more about... you know?" Honey waves a piece of bacon at me.

"Look at her ring," Daria points out. Honey drops everything to ooh and ahh over it. Even Angel looks impressed. I fight the urge to tuck my hand away.

"He's made it clear that I'm his woman," I admit.

Honey claps her hands. "What about the claiming ceremony? Has he said anything about that?"

I shake my head.

"It's supposed to be secret." Honey has a faraway look.

"Which means you know all about it," Daria snarks.

Honey sticks out her tongue at her. "There are conflicting reports. Some say it's in a BDSM club downtown."

"Not at Inferno?" Daria asks.

"No, another place. Club Empire."

Daria nods.

Angel's gone quiet. She's in long sleeves, but she's rubbing her upper arm, where I know she has a snake tattoo. She usually hides the ink with makeup, but I've seen it in the dressing room.

There's a rap on the door.

"I'll get it." Honey hops to her feet. Daria launches out of her chair and dashes to catch up with her.

"Not so fast." She pushes past Honey and calls, "Who is it?"

The familiar voice of the delivery man announces, "I have a delivery for Bunny."

"Bunny?" Honey asks.

"It's okay," I call. "Let him in."

They both open the door and accept the package.

It's a rectangular gift box. Angel helps clear away the candles and knickknacks to make space for it on the coffee table in front of me.

"Open it," Honey squeals.

Inside the box, a thick cream tissue paper holds the scent of lavender and sandalwood. I draw out a short, white dress—a lacy sheath lined with silk.

"Oh gods," Angel murmurs.

Honey half shrieks and covers her mouth. She's thinking this is a wedding dress.

For a second, my heart stops beating.

A cream-colored piece of paper flutters to the floor. Angel catches it and hands it to me.

"For tonight," it reads. It has to be from Jaeger.

I show them the note.

"Tonight? What's tonight?" Daria asks.

"Oh," Honey shrieks again. "I know what it is."

"What?" we all demand.

"He's going to take you to Pandemonium."

Pandemonium. I mouth the word. I've heard it before, at Inferno.

"Where's that?" Daria asks.

"It's an event, not a place," Honey explains. She glances at Angel as if for confirmation, but the dancer is conspicuously silent. "This year, it's at Club Empire. It's a big private party. Typically a masquerade for the kinkiest elite of New Rome. Rumor has it Senator Nero attends. And Rex Roy."

"Who's Rex Roy?" I ask. The name sounds familiar, but I can't remember where I've heard it.

"You don't know who Rex Roy is?" Honey turns wide eyes to me. "The billionaire?

"Oh, right." Now I remember. He's one of the richest men in the nation. I've seen him in the newspapers and on

TV. "Of course, I know him. He and I had tea with the queen just last Thursday."

"Stop." Honey throws a pillow at me and rises with dignity. "I need to powder my nose."

I point her to the nearest bathroom, but she waves me off and heads for my and Jaeger's bedroom so she can use that. She's taking advantage of my offer to snoop.

The second the door closes behind Honey, Daria leans in. "Listen, Elodie, you need to be careful."

Her hushed tone makes me frown. "What?"

"Honey thinks this is a fantasy world. Intrigue, danger... she has stars in her eyes. She's young."

"You're young," I point out, even as I note that the shadows under her eyes look deeper. I look up at Angel, who still hasn't said a word. "We're all young."

"She doesn't understand," Daria says. "This shit is real. Just... be careful."

I bite my lip. If Daria could see the contents of my thoughts, she'd know I'm worried.

Jaeger's been careful to show me a fantasy world consisting of long days in his penthouse watching rom-coms along with expensive clothes and a sexy car. But I know there's another side to his life, a dark side, that pays for all this luxury. He's shown me some of that too—Inferno, his errand to the church, Father Francis, Kaiser. And he's shared his past.

I've tried to ignore Jaeger's mafia side, but it's becoming impossible. I feel like a frog in a pot, slowly being boiled. I'm afraid I'll wake up one day and know everything. Jaeger will pull me into his dark underworld, and I won't be strong enough to survive the monsters that lurk there.

I might be paranoid, but I have a growing premonition

that the dreaded moment is soon. I'm running out of time to figure out how to escape.

The way I'm out-of-my-mind horny from his edging doesn't help.

I cross my legs, ignoring the way my clit cries out for more contact and nod. "I will," I promise her quietly, just before Honey returns from the bathroom to sit back down.

Daria gives me a troubled look but changes the subject. Her warning stays with me. I do need to be careful if I'm stepping into Jaeger's world.

The trouble is, I'm not the one in control.

As if on cue, there's a knock on the front door before it swings open. Jaeger steps in, nodding to us.

"Ladies," he greets us. "Having a good time?"

My friends reply, Honey more enthusiastically than Angel or Daria.

"Excellent." He turns his wolfish grin on me, and I freeze in the middle of reaching for my coffee mug. "Please excuse me and Elodie for a moment." He swings me into his arms and heads toward the bedroom.

"Um, be right back," I call to my friends.

Honey looks delighted. Angel hides a smile.

The bedroom door shuts, and Jaeger lays me on the bed.

"What's this about?" I prop myself to my hands. Jaeger gets down on his knees at the foot of the bed and reaches up to unzip my jeans. He drags them off along with my panties and draws me closer so my legs dangle over his shoulder.

"I'll be quick," he tells me and seals his mouth to my sex.

My hips rise up, and I'm shuddering in no time. He flattens his tongue and batters my clit. I writhe, already hurtling toward an orgasm.

And then he stops. *No!*

"Jaeger?" I struggle up so I can grab onto him, but he's

already pulled away. I'm soaking wet, and he uses my panties to mop up my juices, being careful not to touch me too much.

"Don't cum. Not yet." He keeps re-dressing me, first sliding my legs back into another pair of panties and then my jeans. I whimper, the mere brush of a fresh pair of underwear enough to make my pussy throb.

"Why not?"

"Because I said so." Jaeger cups the back of my neck and kisses me, his face wet. I surrender to him if only to show how much I need him. I'm grasping his shoulders and trying to pull him on top of me when he lifts his head and fixes me with a stern, sexy glare. "If you cum, I'll know. And you will be punished."

I gape at him but can't suppress a flare of excitement at his threat of punishment. "Why?" I ask, too overwhelmed by horniness to be wary. "What's going on?"

He strokes my cheek. "There's a party tonight."

My brain is filled with pink fog, but a light flares in the distance as I make the connection. "Is that why you sent the dress?"

"Yes. You'll come to the party as mine." He's still cupping my cheek, looking supremely satisfied.

I remember what Honey said about Pandemonium being held at a BDSM club. "You mean... your submissive?"

He sets his hand lightly around my throat. "Mmhmm."

The fog clears. The ache in my pussy is enough to make me cranky. "And I'm just supposed to go along with this?" I demand.

Jaeger sticks his face close to mine. "Do you want to cum?"

I growl at him.

He just kisses me again and buttons up my jeans. He gathers me in his arms, and I bury my face in his neck.

"You okay?" he whispers.

I groan in answer. I want to cum. I want answers about tonight's outing, but more than that, I want to cum!

"Love you, bunny," he murmurs and strokes my curls. I rear back to search his face, but there's nothing but calm assurance in his expression.

He loves me?

"And you love me." He sounds sure.

My heart trips over itself. To hide my unsteady breathing, I cross my arms over my chest and narrow my eyes at him. "I do?"

"Yes. You do." He gazes at me with such satisfied assurance I can't meet his eyes.

"I think you're being an asshole." I sound cranky as hell.

"You like that most of all."

I growl, and he chuckles. Another kiss, and he carries me back to my friends.

"Thank you, ladies. Enjoy your visit," he tosses over his shoulder as he leaves.

I sit rigid on the couch, pressing my knees together. For a moment, I'm dizzy. My clit is throbbing, screaming for release. If my friends weren't here, I'd be tempted to risk punishment and squirm out of my jeans to rub one out.

"You okay?" Daria asks.

I press my hands to my cheeks. My skin is burning hot.

I nod slowly.

"Are you sure?" Angel asks. She's rubbing her tattoo, a knowing look on her face.

Love you. And you love me.

I shake my head.

"Did you ask him about tonight?" Honey asks, breathless. "Is it the ceremony?"

The ceremony... the dress. *You'll come to the party as mine.* "I don't know. He didn't mention a ceremony, not exactly. We discussed... other things."

Honey giggles. Even Daria has a smile on her face. They know exactly what went on behind closed doors, and I can't bring myself to care.

I stare at the front door, wishing Jaeger would return.

He wants to make you his elita.

"I don't know what I'm doing," I tell them.

"Are you in love with him?" Honey asks.

I put my hands on my cheeks. I'm burning up. "He's Fraternitas."

"So?" Honey snorts. She starts to say more, and Angel holds out her hand to stop her.

"If he wasn't in the mafia, would you want him?" Angel is sitting up straight, studying me.

I gnaw on my lower lip. "It doesn't matter. He won't let me leave."

Honey's eyes go wide, and Daria shakes her head, but Angel doesn't seem phased. "Do you want to leave?"

"I don't know."

"Are you afraid to stay?" Angel keeps digging. Honey looks from her to me, drinking in the interrogation.

"Gods, Angel." I blow out a breath. "Maybe."

"Well then, there's only one question you need to ask yourself. What would you do if you weren't afraid?"

I glare at her and then Daria, who's silent, biting her lip. *Be careful.*

And all the while, my sex pulses with need. Because deep down, I'm turned on by danger.

Stupid bunny, hopping right up to the wolf.

But it's more than that. Jaeger is my safe place. Everything he's done to care for me has lured me in a little bit more.

I need him. I crave him. I want him and want to take care of him. He's had so little, and yet he's given me so much.

I want to give him my everything.

And that scares me most of all.

I sink back into the couch, wanting to pull the cashmere throw over my head.

Honey waves as if clearing the air. "Enough of all this. You have a date tonight. I have two hours before my shift. So we're going to get you ready. Hair, makeup, nails. The works."

"Okay," I agree weakly. I may as well do something to take my mind off my aching pussy.

Jaeger shows up right as my friends are leaving. By then, I'm desperate and holding myself together with fraying threads. The sun is sinking, filling the penthouse with golden light.

I hear Angel and Honey greet him at the door and his rumbling reply. Then it shuts, and there's only the sound of him heading my way. Finally.

I'm on the bed, already dolled up. I put on the dress so they could do my makeup and hair. Honey did something called an "airbrush" effect. Angel even put makeup on my arms, because apparently that's something people do when their dress is sleeveless. I'm afraid to move in case I mess up all their hard work.

He stops in the doorway, cast in shadow.

My breath comes faster at the sight of him. My pussy is dripping, soaking the gusset of my panties, and my nipples are swollen, ripe berries begging to be plucked.

He's got me trained. I'm on a hair-trigger, ready for him

to fuck me. I need him. Sitting all day, waiting for him to come back and finish what he started, was torture.

I hold out my arms as if to say, "Well?" I'm primped and polished, all for him. I'd give anything to throw this dress off and put my hands between my legs. Even the satiny lining of the dress is too much stimulation.

Then he walks into the room, into the light, and I almost cum from the sight. He's in a tuxedo, all white, the exact color of my dress. The pristine color draws attention to the perfect symmetry of his face and the dark ink peeking out from under his cuffs and collar.

"You look beautiful, bunny," he says gruffly. Then he takes in my stunned reaction. "Do you like what you see?"

I'm still speechless, so I nod. There's something about the sophisticated trappings of a suit that enhances the feral quality of his long hair and tattoos. He looks elegant and dangerous. More dangerous because of the refined pretense.

Jaeger can be gentle, but he's not a gentleman. An appeal to chivalry won't save me.

He says he loves me, but I can't underestimate him.

"So beautiful." He extends a finger and brushes a curl from the side of my face. "Hmmm." His eyes narrow as he takes in my heavy makeup. Honey was going to repaint my face with fake freckles after she coated the real ones with concealer, but I wouldn't let her.

"You're only missing one thing." Planting a hand on my chest, he presses me back to the bed. I lie down, watching him warily. The last time he did this to me, he left me on edge and wanting.

What is he going to do now? My heart is rioting in my chest, but I lie still because I want to know what happens next.

He pulls something from his pocket and slides the silk

folds of the dress up to my waist. I make a noise of protest, and he shushes me.

"These are for you." He shows me two silver balls. They're the size of large marbles, and they knock together in his palm with a clunking sound.

My question of what I'll do with them dies when he eases aside my thong and sets one of them at my entrance. He holds my gaze, the dark of his pupil swallowing the blue as he inserts the balls inside me. As wet as I am, they side in easily. They're heavier than they look and rub against my sensitive inner walls with their delicious weight.

"You must clench around them to keep them in." He runs a thumb up my seam, and I clench down, only to moan when the movement makes the balls move inside me. "If you drop one..." He leaves the threat hanging.

"Why?" I gasp as the balls roll forward, stimulating me deeply.

"I want you like this. Wet and needy for me."

I'm shaking my head. The balls stimulate but don't satisfy me. They're not large enough. They're only enough to tease me. "I can't do this."

"You can. You will." Jaeger helps me sit up on the edge of the bed and straightens my lovely dress. He touches my chin, tipping my head back. "You must."

I pant, overcome.

He turns my head this way and that, studying my face. "Hmm," he peers at my cheeks. "There is one more thing I require."

He runs a thumb over my cheek, and I pull away.

"Careful." I'm half-crazed with arousal, but my friends worked hard to get me all dolled up. "You'll smear my makeup."

He stands and lifts me, not picking me up but lowering me to my knees. "Your ankle okay?" he asks.

"Yes?" I stare up at him.

He looms over me, his head haloed in light but his face shrouded in darkness. His white slacks are tented.

I shift on my knees. "What—"

He opens his pants and offers his cock to me.

"Open your mouth." He pinches my nose, but it's unnecessary. I've already tilted my head back and opened for him. I'm hungry for any sort of sexual stimulation. I keep my eyes on him, wondering what he's up to. His cock is thick and meaty, filling my mouth.

He transfers both of his hands to either side of my head and forces me down. I choke, but his hips tilt, driving his length deeper. The head of his cock hits the back of my throat, and I gag. I slap at his waist, pushing so I can breathe.

Finally, he lets me up. I gasp, panting for air. My eyes are streaming.

"Again." He grips my face, guiding me down again. I take a deep breath this time so I'm braced for when he presses in, gagging me. His cock swells, cutting off my air. I work my tongue, trying to stimulate him to cum faster. But he keeps pushing until he's knocking on the back of my throat.

I dig my fingers into his white pants. Am I pulling him closer or pushing him away? I have no idea. All I know is I can't breathe. My body is overheating, and the pressure in my sex grows.

This is going to end, one way or another.

He pulls out, and I sag forward. I would fall, but he's holding me up as I cough and hack. Drool drips from my lips. I wipe it away. There goes my lipstick. Tears stream out of my eyes.

"There," he murmurs. He strokes my face, smearing the

foundation and concealer further. He swipes his thumbs across the apples of my cheeks, and they come away black. My mascara must be bleeding down my face.

My makeup is ruined. All those layers of foundation and concealer, gone.

He pulls out a handkerchief and wipes the rest of my tears away.

"I can see your freckles again," he says. With his blond hair haloed in the dying light, he's as beautiful as an angel.

"What?" I croak. My throat is raw from the throat-fucking.

"I wanted to see your freckles." His touch is reverent. He caresses the skin that's been washed clean from my tears. "Now we can leave."

13

E *lodie*

By the time the Lykan pulls up to Club Empire, my brain is mush. Every time I forget the sensation in my pussy, the balls move, and I clamp my muscles down, awakening my arousal all over again. My nipples are hard and pointy, chafed by the silk of my dress. I want to grab Jaeger and devour him.

It's not possible to be this horny and survive.

I keep glancing at Jaeger's lap, where his pants are tight. I haven't cum, but neither has he. Not even when he used my mouth. He's been denying himself alongside me.

It doesn't make me feel better.

Club Empire isn't what I'd expected. For one thing, it's not flashy at all. There's no sign on the front door announcing the kinky delights inside. It's in a black building with a formal entrance fit for any sort of business.

I've heard rumors about this place, about the platinum membership that costs a hundred thousand dollars a year—or was it a month?—and about the playrooms where the rich and famous go to live out their deepest, darkest fantasies.

And now I'm here. With a member of Fraternitas.

The old me is wondering how in the hell I got here.

The new me is too horny to think straight. I guess that was Jaeger's plan all along.

The valet comes up to open Jaeger's door, but Jaeger holds up a hand for him to wait.

Jaeger pulls a set of white masks out of his pocket. Mine is lace to match my dress, and his is plain. He ties the ribbon around my head.

"You ready?" he asks me.

I swallow, staring at the red carpet lining the sidewalk leading into the club. A couple in fine evening wear strolls up and disappears inside.

He takes my hand, and I grip it, hard.

"I'll be with you every step of the way," he promises. It should calm my trepidation, but it stokes it instead.

What am I getting myself into?

Jaeger opens his door and tosses his keys to a valet before coming around to pick me up. Before he does, he says, "One more thing." He stoops to fasten a white ribbon around my throat.

"What..." I go to tug at it, and he catches my hand.

"Do not remove it."

"What is it? What does it mean?"

His eyes are dark, framed by the white mask. "It means you're untouchable."

"What?"

"Everyone can look, but if they try to claim what's mine..." He traces the ribbon collaring my neck. "They die."

I suck in a breath. He settles his hand around my throat, squeezing lightly. I feel the imprint of his grip even after he takes his hand away.

I cling to him as he carries me into the club and a cloud of expensive perfume. He sweeps through the foyer, passing the other guests, and heads upstairs, clearly familiar with the place.

I'm grateful he's carrying me. My ankle is wrapped, and I'm wearing soft silk slippers that match the dress. I could probably walk, but it's nice to have Jaeger take charge, even though the movement makes the silver balls roll back and forth inside me.

I clamp my legs together. My clit pulses to a silent beat.

Upstairs is a bar, smelling faintly of cigar smoke and cloves. The mahogany booths and velvet curtains remind me of Inferno. Against one wall is a long bar of polished wood, with unlabeled liquor bottles backlit against the mirror. The liquid in the bottles ranges from every shade of whiskey—rich amber to pale gold.

Jaeger sets me on a padded stool next to a high table in the far corner and heads for the bar. I keep still, becoming one with the shadows. The place is full of people in expensive finery, billionaires and socialites here to see and be seen.

Fortunately, no one looks at me. I check everyone's hands, looking for skull rings, but only find two.

The men wearing them are in a booth, tucked into the shadows. They're both in black tuxes, blending in with the rest of the party. One of the men is fair-haired, with a long, lean build that speaks of the fit and muscular body underneath.

The other man is shorter but built like a boxer. He's dark-haired with deep shadows under his eyes. He looks comfortable in his tux, but his hands are tattooed with the jaw and teeth of a skull, and his skull ring is unlike any I've ever seen. Diamonds glitter in the skull's eye sockets and on the skull's head is a crown.

I'm staring. At members of Fraternitas, no less. I tear my eyes away. Jaeger is still at the bar, leaning in to speak to the bartender.

I sense someone's eyes on me, and I turn back.

The shorter man has risen out of the booth but pauses to stare at me. His dark gaze narrows on my neck. I shrink back when I realize he's looking at the ribbon Jaeger placed there. His expression is blank, but panic rises in me. I get the sense that this man's blank expression is the last thing many have seen before they die.

The second man rises and stands with the dark-haired man. I recognize his pale, narrow face and colorless eyes. It's St. James. He raises his chin, acknowledging me.

My heart stops beating. My hand goes to my throat in an automatic gesture to protect my vulnerable neck. These men are apex predators, and they've clocked me. The urge to rip off the ribbon and throw it away is strong, but I'm in Jaeger's world now. I can't be weak.

I lower my hand and clench my fists, and the moment passes. The man with skulls on his hands breaks the stare and heads for the door with St. James following him.

St. James is high up in the ranks of Fraternitas. Everyone I know of follows his orders.

So, who was the man with the crowned skull on his ring? And why was he looking at me like that?

Jaeger appears at my side, holding two glasses filled with

red liquid. I relax when his big body blocks my view of the rest of the room.

"Good girl," he praises me. I realize I'm fingering the ribbon at my neck again and drop my hand. "You're doing well," he adds, making me think he saw the whole thing.

"Who were those men?" I ask. I should be smart and keep quiet, but I can't help it.

"That was St. James. You know him." Jaeger answers right away. He did see it. He brought me here to be seen. "And the man with him is Damien. The Devil."

And now I know the man called "the Devil" has a real name, and it's Damien. Great. Honey will be ecstatic.

Be careful, Daria's warning comes to me.

"Why did you bring me here?" I ask. I have to know. Ignorance won't save me anymore.

"Tonight is a very special night. We're here to watch a ceremony binding one of my brothers to his *elita*."

I squeeze my legs together. I'm so desperate to cum I might submit to a ceremony. "Just watch?"

"Just watch."

I don't know whether to be relieved or disappointed.

"It'll be okay, bunny. I'll be with you the whole time. Here." He sets a glass to my lips. "It's juice," he tells me when I hesitate. "Nothing alcoholic."

I take a sip, and he's right. Something sparkling is in it that makes my tongue tingle, and there's a complexity to the flavor like they added a shrub of some sort.

Jaeger's drink looks the same.

"You can drink," I tell him. We're in a bar, after all.

"I'll drink what you drink," he says, and even with my aching core and the nervousness gripping me, his solidarity warms me through and through.

I lean close to him, and the balls shift inside me, making

me dizzy. I end up clutching his arm, my forehead pressed to his shoulder.

"What's wrong?"

I swallow. "The balls... they're..." I can't explain how I feel. I gaze at him in a silent plea for mercy.

"My poor bunny. Being so good, suffering for me." He strokes my face, and I bite back a moan. "Don't worry. You can cum soon."

"When?" My cunt is swollen. One touch could get me off.

"When I say so. Not a moment before." I shut my eyes, and he whispers in my ear. "Do this for me, bunny, and I'll give you the world."

When I open my eyes again, the bar is clearing out. People are drifting toward the door.

"Come." Jaeger tosses back his drink. He offers me the rest of mine and when I refuse, he downs that as well. "The festivities will start soon."

We head back downstairs, this time by elevator. The doors open into a packed room, several stories high and lit by a massive chandelier overhead.

The elite of New Rome are here, in tuxedos and ball gowns and a few in catsuits of patent leather. Weaving through the crowd are club submissives in black and red corsets, teetering on red-soled stilettos.

Jaeger carries me through the crowd, heading to the far wall where there's a large gilt chair set on a small platform. Still holding me, Jaeger sinks onto the red velvet cushions. The elevated height puts us head and shoulders above the crowd, and I can see everything.

A few heads turn our way, and I jolt upright in Jaeger's arms. Most people are wearing plain black or white masks or more elaborate ones glittering with jewels. But not these men.

They're wearing different sorts of skull masks. Some black, some white, some silver. The effect is chilling.

"Jaeger," I whisper, more to make contact with him than anything. I stare across the room at a huge guy in an executioner's hood painted with a skull. His face and hair are covered, but there's a spiderweb tattoo on his hand.

It's Kaiser. And he's glaring at me.

"Don't be afraid," Jaeger murmurs. "Smile and wave." I do, but not being afraid is easier said than done.

In the center of the room are more people in different sorts of skull masks, gathering around another platform. They're all wearing skull rings.

The masked man closest to us has shucked off his suit jacket, showing off his shirtless torso. He's in a black vest that leaves his burly arms bare, and his arms are wrapped around a tall, slim woman. It takes me a moment to place her, but then I realize—it's Odette. I'd recognize her perfect dancer's posture anywhere. She's elegant in a dress of midnight blue, which makes her brown skin glow. Her ballerina bun showcases her graceful neck.

The last time I saw Odette, she was wearing a black ribbon around her throat, a dark blue jewel hanging from it. Now, it's been replaced by a metal collar, either silver or white gold, with what looks like the same blue jewel. The gemstone matches the one in the man's ring.

It's just like Honey had told me. I wish she were here so she could explain what I'm seeing.

Now that I've noticed Odette, I can pick out more figures besides the men in masks. Some are wearing black ribbons around their neck. Some of the ribbons are white.

One woman is wearing a red ribbon around her throat. She's to my far right, kneeling near the wall. She has dyed burgundy hair and a black ball gag in her mouth, and her arms are secured behind her in a red leather binder. She's in a matching red leather bustier that leaves her breasts exposed. Her nipples are pierced and linked with a chain. The masked man beside her is holding a leash that leads to the chain.

My breath catches. Jaeger notices and leans in. "Like what you see?"

I swallow. I should look away, but I've just noticed the woman's eyes. They're open, but both the iris and the pupil are a uniform black. She must be wearing contact lenses that black out her vision, in addition to the rest of her bondage.

"Bunny?" Jaeger's waiting for me to admit my interest.

I give him a shake of my head and turn away. But I can't deny my pussy is throbbing harder.

The room is growing full as more people stream in. Murmurs sound from around the room, but when St. James steps onto the center platform, everyone falls silent.

"Dearly beloved," he intones and chuckles erupt like it's a joke. "We're gathered here for the commitment ceremony of two of our cherished members. The one called Asmodeus, and the one he will claim. Sarah."

A man in a silver skull mask steps onto the platform. He's shirtless, with a red dragon inked across his rippling muscles. I can't make out his ring or any other features besides his long black hair.

"Sarah." Asmodeus holds out a hand and helps a young blonde woman onto the platform. She's in a short, white dress. It's simple and almost see-through, more like a silk slip than a dress.

A lot like the one I'm wearing now.

Once she's on the platform, Asmodeus points to a spot in front of him. I suck in a breath, my belly quivering. Biting her lip, Sarah goes down to her knees. She gazes up at the masked figure looming over her, her eyes wide with expectation and fear.

Her hand drifts up to touch the ribbon around her neck. It's black.

"Hands behind your back," Asmodeus commands, loud enough for everyone to hear. Sarah obeys, and he leans in, saying something more that the rest of the room can't hear.

"Do you like this, bunny?" Jaeger shifts so he can whisper right in my ear. "Does it make you wet?" He doesn't wait for my answer, just reaches under my dress, between my legs and checks. I suck in a breath, my stomach tightening. The balls move inside me. I grab his wrist, but I can't stop him from touching me.

"Jaeger, there are people here."

"No one is watching us." He starts stroking me, and my body, orgasm-starved as it is, crows with excitement. I cling to his arm, more to steady myself than to stall him.

His finger finds my clit and circles it. A little more pressure, and I'll cum.

St. James is announcing more to the room, but my ears are filled with a buzzing sound. Even as my attention is on Jaeger's finger, I can't take my eyes off the proceedings.

A club submissive steps onto the platform and goes down on one knee, offering up a pillow with a silver collar on it.

Asmodeus steps behind Sarah and removes the black ribbon. There's a jewel on it that I didn't notice before, but I can't see the color. He slides the jewel off the ribbon and takes up the metal collar.

Jaeger bites the tip of my ear, and I shudder. I'm so close, but he seems to know that. His finger retreats.

"Don't come. Not yet."

To take my mind off the intense ache between my legs, I ask, "What's happening?"

On stage, Asmodeus has threaded the jewel onto the metal collar. St. James orders Sarah to present her neck for collaring. She gathers up her hair.

"He is claiming her as his *elita*. His chosen one. She will belong to him in every way, and all of Fraternitas will be loyal to her as she is to him."

And is this what you want us to do? It's on the tip of my tongue to ask, but I just watch as Asmodeus fixes the collar around Sarah's neck. Bending, he grips her blonde hair and draws her head back so he can kiss her.

The men in masks pump their fists to the sky. "Fraternitas." They chant. Jaeger secures me in one arm and joins them, shouting, "Fraternitas. Fraternitas."

Their shouts die away.

Asmodeus is already helping Sarah down from the stage.

St. James raises his hands for quiet. "Ladies and gentlemen, welcome to Pandemonium."

The room plunges into darkness. Music blasts from the corners, a deep bass beat that makes the hair on my arms rise. Colored lights crisscross the space, turning it into a dance floor. Figures in the crowd glow with neon threads. The corsets worn by the club employees are outlined in green and pink glow-in-the-dark piping. A few of them are holding floggers that glow red.

One by one, door-shaped arches light up on the walls to the left and right of us. Four stories of rooms with see-through sections reveal the people in each room and the activities they're engaged in. Bodies twined together, kissing, embracing, fucking.

I shouldn't watch, but I can't tear my eyes away.

Jaeger's hands roam over me. My overheated blood, set to simmer, starts to boil.

"Jaeger..."

"Shhhh, bunny. Give in to me." His hand covers my breast. I lean back into him, arching into his touch.

At the closest door, a masked figure presses a smaller person against the wall and rams into them from behind. In the next, a figure stands fixed to a St. Andrew's cross with their limbs splayed, while a second figure holds a whip, and a third fists a large, prominent cock or dildo jutting out between their legs.

Jaeger slips the strap off my shoulders, drawing my dress down so he can bare my chest. I struggle, caught between trying to push him away and pulling him closer. He pins me against him, securing my wrists behind me and turning me sideways across his lap, bending me back against the arm of the chair. The position allows me to see the room while he plays with my bare breasts. He bows his head to take my nipple into his mouth.

Electricity shoots through me, making me gasp. I'm pinned and helpless, watching people writhe on the dance floor in front of us. The room has cleared out somewhat as couples, throuples, and pods go upstairs to private rooms. The rest of the crowd has turned into a mosh pit, with a few couples in a clinch right in front of us. Two men have a lady locked between them, and one of them kisses her while the other unzips her ballgown, stripping her as I watch.

Jaeger sets his teeth at my nipple and bites down. I jerk as if I've been shocked.

A young man in a white lace mask like mine runs from

another man in a gold mask. The pursued looks back at his pursuer but trips and falls. Two figures in long-beaked plague masks emerge out of the shadows. They grab the young man and hold him so the man in the gold mask can take hold of him and drag him away.

Another throuple, consisting of a tall man in the center, who's leading two half- naked submissives by their leashes, strolls past me. The submissives are in chastity devices—one in a cock cage and the other in a smooth silver belt—and their hands are bound behind their backs. A tremor goes through me when I realize I know the man in the middle. It's Atticus. He winks at me and turns to tug his pets to him and accept their worshipful kisses.

The room has turned into an orgy right in front of my eyes. The men in the skull masks have disappeared, or they've taken off their disguises. I search the room for them or their collared partners but don't see them.

I have bigger things to worry about. Jaeger's kissing my breasts, but his hand between my legs has stilled.

I push at Jaeger's head, and when he raises it, I cup his cheeks and kiss him. He hums, leaning into the kiss, bowing me back over his arm. His lips slide to the corner of my mouth and drag downward. He sucks on my nipple, and I cry out.

I'm shaking with the need to cum. My inner muscles clench around the weighted balls, and arousal surges through me, making me delirious. I'm so close.

Jaeger raises his head, laser-thin lights crisscrossing his face. "Do you want to cum like this? In front of everyone?"

I shake my head, but my hips are surging upward, seeking his touch. I might not have a choice.

He grips my pussy lips so hard I cry out. It hurts so good. "Beg me, Elodie."

"Jaeger, please." I'm sobbing. So overwhelmed by the lights, the pulsing music, everything about this night.

He releases my pussy, and the pain dies away, along with my hopes for an orgasm.

Jaeger stands up with me in his arms but turns and sets me down on the chair. I shiver without his warmth, feeling lost.

He leans in, cupping the back of my neck. "Are you going to be good for me?" His fingers twist in my curls, tugging a little, sparking a stinging sensation along my hairline.

The rest of the room, the booming bass and flashing lights, all fade away. There's only the two of us.

I lick my lips. "I want to cum."

"Soon." He squeezes my knee with his free hand.

"I hate you," I tell him. He smirks, but I'm seized with the need to tell him the truth. I catch his face between my palms. "I didn't mean it. Jaeger, I..." I stare into his stormy eyes, unable to say the rest. *I crave you. I want more time with you in the penthouse, cuddling on the couch. I want to be the one you whisper secrets to in the dark.*

But I'm afraid.

His gaze softens. "I know." He brushes his lips over mine. "I love you, too."

He knows.

A sense of peace falls over me. Jaeger isn't the man I would've imagined falling for. I didn't choose him; he chose me. But every man in my life has left. Maybe a man who won't let me go is what I need.

"I love you," I tell him because I can't go another second without telling him.

He pulls away, looming over me, and a chill falls over me. Something's about to happen.

"You need to be brave now. And very, very good." He

blankets my eyes with a blindfold, plunging me into darkness.

Panic makes me thrash. "What—"

He sets a finger to my lips. "Not another word. Or I'll need to gag you." He waits for my nod and gathers my hands, binding them together with some sort of soft rope.

Then he fits something over my head. Something covers my ears, muffling the sounds around me but not quite silencing the pulsing music.

I fight another flash of fear. He's taken away my vision, my ability to use my hands, and now my hearing. I remember the woman in the armbinder with the red ribbon.

I open my mouth and remember what he said about the gag. Still, I squirm when he touches me. He lifts one of the soft covers off my ear long enough to say, "Shh, bunny. Don't struggle. Save your strength. You will need it."

Then he replaces the covering, leaving me caught in my own dark world. I can only flex my wrists in the bindings as he picks me up and carries me somewhere. He has something planned. I don't know where we're going. I can only guess—upstairs, to the bar? Or into one of those illuminated rooms to put on a show?

I only know I'll be with him. He's promised to stay by my side.

I told him I love him, and I mean it. I don't know when he became the one person in the world I can lean on.

I only hope he doesn't let me fall.

～

Jaeger

. . .

THE BASS BEAT and sounds of dancers fade into the distance as I leave the ballroom and head into the bowels of the building. There's another secret elevator at the end of a hall. This one doesn't budge until I give it a voice command and angle my hand for a hidden sensor to scan my ring.

And then we're descending, far below Club Empire, to a place only Fraternitas knows. Into the Abyss.

Growing up on the streets, you quickly learn of the secret passages under the city. There's a whole world under New Rome—old pipes, subway systems, and underground rooms. It didn't take us long to realize we could have free run of the place. When you're small and insignificant, no one notices when you disappear. It's a street kid's greatest weakness—and our greatest strength.

Father Francis taught us world history and how empires rise and fall. Damien and St. James were the first to understand that whoever rules the underworld rules the streets. First, with smuggling routes, then the illegal gambling and fight clubs, and, when Fraternitas had obtained enough wealth and control to make us powerful, the whole city.

Now we rule above ground, but we've never forgotten the place that made us. It's ours to lose, so we must keep it and use it for our most secret meetings and rituals.

And now I've brought Elodie here. My brothers need to know what she means to me, and she needs to understand what Fraternitas truly is. The best way to do that is to show her and show them all.

I stride quickly through the dank tunnel, following the lost light. I know the way by heart and reach a section lined with grime-covered subway tiles and turn right. The way grows darker. I'm in the oldest part of the city, long forgotten.

Elodie is shivering in her thin dress, but she doesn't

make a sound. It's not fair to put her through this, but she has to know what Fraternitas is. I've dedicated my life to them. They took my violent impulses and gave them purpose. And now they've given me Elodie.

I'm breaking our greatest laws by bringing her here, but St. James is the one who set all this in motion. I've never gotten a birthday gift before, and he gave her to me. On the streets, the first lesson you learn is to hold on to what you have. He learned that lesson just like I did. He can't blame me when I refuse to give her up.

Voices echo in the distance. I'm getting closer to my destination.

Light spills up a set of gray-green steps. I descend into the brilliant blaze, moving slowly until my eyes adjust. We're on a narrow ledge, a balcony of sorts, overlooking our ritual space. Damien calls our meetings "church," and it's both ironic and accurate. This is where we meet, plan, and vow our allegiance to one another. On nights like tonight, it's where we spill blood.

I sit down on a low ledge that will give us a view of the proceedings, with Elodie in my lap, rigid.

"You must be quiet," I warn her and lift the blindfold to direct her terrified eyes to the dark sanctuary below us. "The ceremony is about to begin."

ELODIE

I CAN TELL the moment we're not in Club Empire anymore. The smell gives it away. It's the smell of dark underground places. Mold and sewer drains. There's a clammy chill mixed with random blasts of heat and the faraway, screeching and rumbling sounds of a subway.

I huddle against Jaeger's strong chest, hoping he doesn't set me down. The farther he walks, the more my fear grows.

Then he carries me down a set of stairs to a warmer space, where the air holds a faint trace of a smokey scent, like incense.

There's another scent under the smell of smoke and spices. Something fetid with a metallic edge.

The blindfold lifts, and for a moment, my senses are overwhelmed with light. I blink and take in Jaeger's features. He murmurs a warning to be quiet and something about a ceremony. Panic rushes over my skin, chasing away the chill.

Jaeger brought me to a cavernous space lit by candles. We're up in the corner, overlooking the rest of the huge rectangular room. It's like we're in a booth at a theater, and all the action is happening below us.

I peer over the ledge and bite back a scream. The room is filled with people, and every one of them is wearing a skull mask. Some are in street clothes. Some are wearing black robes. The sinister effect is the same. They fill the room, taking their places in rows and rows of benches. It's so quiet I can hear a candle guttering in its holder.

No wonder Jaeger told me to be quiet. I don't think anyone knows that he and I are watching. I don't think I'm supposed to be here. I can't see from this vantage point, but I'd bet my hundred thousand dollars that all the figures are wearing rings.

The walls and floor are all black stone, shining like obsidian and reflecting the amber-gold light. There are fireplaces built right into the walls, and a strip of gas flames runs all the way around the room.

At the front of the room is an open space lined with

standing candelabra and a stone circle filled with dark water —a small pool.

And I realize what this place reminds me of. The smell of incense, the rows of benches laid out like pews, the ceremonial space at the front of the room: it's all a depraved imitation of a church. Alcoves line the walls, just like at St. Xavier's, but instead of figures of the saints, each alcove holds a skull mask, spotlit with eerie amber light.

In the altar area at the front of the room, a group of robed figures gather. I shouldn't be staring—*I shouldn't be here*—but I can't look away.

Among the group, one stands out. Blonde hair, pale skin. It's Sarah in her new silver collar. In the darkness, her white dress shines like a beacon, and she's being led by a silver leash that's held by the man with dragon tattoos. Asmodeus.

A shorter man steps forward in a black mask stylized into a skull and wearing a crown. He raises his arms and chants something in a language I don't recognize.

"That's Damien." The ghost of Jaeger's whisper reaches my ears. "And St. James." He points to a robed figure blending into the shadows behind the pool. "You know Asmodeus. He's one of the Seven the Devil appointed as his generals."

Oh gods. I don't want to know all this. There's another robed person beside Damien, sitting in a wheelchair. They have a slighter frame, and when they offer up a ceremonial dagger, the sleeves of their robes fall away to show colorful tattoos. Green vines with thorns, weeping roses the color of blood. I recognize the tattoos. I've seen them before on the woman who runs Inferno.

"Lucy," Jaeger confirms my suspicions. I flex my forearms in their bondage, wishing I could run.

Another woman is standing nearby, a hood keeping her face in shadow.

"That's the Devil's woman," Jaeger's murmur stirs my hair. "His elita. I'd tell you her name, but he'd kill me. He's extremely protective of her identity."

The ceremony continues with the Devil and Lucy leading. Asmodeus leads Sarah to the head of the pool. Lucy hands him a goblet, and he orders Sarah to drink, holding the cup to her mouth. She's shaking, but she drinks and then holds the cup for him to drink.

Then he uses the dagger to slice her palm and his, and they exchange some sort of vows. Another robed figure steps forward to lead them in this, his voice deep and level as he recites the Latin phrases. The words bounce off the walls but are meaningless to me. It's clear the ceremony is as formal as a marriage, but in this upside-down world, who knows what sort of vows are being spoken?

But I know I've heard that voice before. The man speaking is hidden under a deep hood, but I can imagine him in my head: bearded and in a simple cassock, wearing a wooden cross.

Father Francis. Why is the priest here?

A door slams open, echoing in the space. I jump, and Jaeger hugs me tight. "Watch," he says.

Two men in executioner hoods drag someone forward. Their captive is a man in a suit. He's gagged and struggling, his hair standing on end as he thrashes in their arms. They muscle him forward and force him to his knees near the pool in front of the priest and the Devil. Both officiants step back, leaving only Sarah and Asmodeus.

Sarah steps in front of the man, who fights harder when he sees her. Asmodeus moves to help hold him down and bend him back over the pool.

My insides turn to lead. I don't know what's going to happen, but I have the feeling it's not going to be good.

Lucy rolls her wheelchair forward and hands Sarah a dagger. Silver glints as she turns it over in her hands. She looks so frail in her simple white dress.

But her face is calm when she steps forward, gripping the knife. A tremor runs through me, and Jaeger holds me fast.

She leans in and says something to the man. He shakes his head but can't move much more than that. Asmodeus rips the man's shirt open, baring an expanse of pale flesh, and nods to Sarah.

With both hands, she raises the knife high and slams it into the victim's chest.

14

E *lodie*

BLOOD SPRAYS, spattering Sarah's solemn face.

I grit my teeth so hard they ache, fighting a scream. I cringe against Jaeger, my stomach full of acid.

Death doesn't come quickly. Sarah's strength wasn't enough to push the knife deep enough. The man's throat strains as he screams into his gag. He tries to move, but the Fraternitas members holding him are strong enough to make sure he doesn't budge.

It's Asmodeus who ends it. He moves behind Sarah, reaching around her to take hold of the blade, his large hands covering Sarah's smaller ones. His muscles strain as he uses his strength to shove the knife all the way in.

The victim's head lolls on his shoulders. He convulses, and the men holding him release him, letting him fall into the pool. Dark blood wells up around the dagger and pours from the wound, blending with the water.

Sarah steps back with clenched hands that are red to the wrist. Her white dress is bright with blood.

Asmodeus turns to her. He touches her face and takes a handful of blonde hair into his fist. He leaves traces of red everywhere he touches.

"Together in life. Bound by death," the priest intones. Asmodeus leads Sarah to the side. They grip each other's hands over a silver bowl, and Lucy pours a goblet of bloody water over their joined hands, filling the bowl.

"Courage, little demon," he tells her, and she jerks her head in a nod. Her blonde hair hangs in clumps, the strands dark red where they've soaked up the blood.

"The ritual includes blood, water, and fire," Jaeger whispers, and I jolt. I've almost forgotten he's here. "We commit ourselves to each other and Fraternitas."

I bite my lip, remembering his brand.

"Sarah is claimed, and now she is bound to Fraternitas as much as Asmodeus bound her to him."

Because she's complicit, I realize. She's committed murder in front of all of them.

The masked men are fishing the body out of the water now. I can't watch anymore.

I face Jaeger. "Why did you show me this?" My voice is barely a whisper.

He picks me up and carries me up the stairs. It's a relief to leave, but as he carries me down a dark tunnel, I lose it.

I wriggle, wrenching myself out of his arms. My arms are tied together, but my feet are free. He lets me down, and I stumble on the cold stone. The balls fall from my sex, bouncing and rolling across the floor, but I barely notice.

I half run, half limp away from Jaeger and everything

he's brought me to. But it's dark, and I don't know the way. And Jaeger never had any trouble hunting me.

I end up in a dimly lit room built of polished stone. There are markings on the wall with names etched in the marble, each labeled with a skull. It's a mausoleum, a place for the Fraternitas dead.

Jaeger's shadow fills the doorway before he steps in.

"You wanted me to see this," I babble. "You brought me here, made me watch. And now I'm complicit, too."

Jaeger stalks forward, and I tilt my head up to him. "But it's more than that, isn't it? If they know I know, and I run, they'll hunt me down." By them, I mean his brothers, Fraternitas.

"Yes." He gestures behind him. "That's what happens to people who know too much. We drag them here. To the Abyss."

My legs fail me, and I fall, but he catches me before I hit the floor.

The hunter has captured me, but this isn't a game anymore.

"I can't do this," I choke.

"You can. You're strong enough." He presses me against the wall and frees a hand to cup between my legs. "I'm going to keep you, bunny." His feral eyes are all I see. "You know too much, and now you can never leave."

I shake my head, too frightened to speak.

"I knew it the night in the woods when it was just the two of us. No society, no civilization, no pretense. You showed me the core of you, everything else stripped away. You were fierce." He's stroking me, and despite all that's happened, my arousal flares. I'm soaking his fingers. "You want me. Saying yes to this is saying yes to yourself." He leans into me, trapping me between his hard body and the wall.

I close my eyes, but I can't escape his touch.

He wants me in his world. He won't take no for an answer.

I cup my throat and feel the ribbon around my neck. Tear at it. "What is this, really? What does it mean?"

"It means you belong to me."

My hips surge against his hand, my body begging for an orgasm.

"Tell me the truth, Elodie. Tell me, and you can cum." His lips at my ear send goosebumps running down my back. "Tell me about the man you want to kill most of all."

"What?" The waters are closing over my head. I'm going under.

"Is it your ex?" Jaeger asks.

"No." I can't. I can't do this. But I'm drowning in him, and I don't even care.

"Tell me." Jaeger twists his fingers, driving them deep inside me. The pressure in my skull increases, and my limbs start to shake. My mouth opens, and I hear myself say, "He was my professor."

"Good bunny. You'll give me his name."

And I do.

Jaeger grips my throat and rams his fingers home. As my orgasm breaks, he squeezes my neck, cutting off my oxygen. It makes me spiral higher.

And then he's inside me, hitching me against him as he impales me on his cock. He slams into me, and my world narrows to the blue fire in his eyes. He releases his death grip on my throat, and I'm no longer drowning. I'm flying to a place only he can send me.

JAEGER

IT'S a long way back to Empire from the Abyss. We're almost to the hidden elevator when a shadow falls in my path. Kaiser. He's been following me, but now that he's let me see him, I know he wants to talk.

He's still wearing his executioner's hood. His eyes flick down to Elodie, passed out in my arms. "She shouldn't be here."

I don't argue with him. I knew I was breaking the rules before I forced her to watch our most secret ritual.

"The Devil will find out."

"Will you tell him, brother?" I ask and walk past him without waiting for an answer.

He's only telling me what I already know. Tonight was the beginning of the end. When the Devil finds out what I've done, he'll pass judgment. I might be a dead man walking, depending on what he decides.

One way or another, the countdown has begun.

ELODIE

WHEN I COME AWAKE in bed, morning light is streaming under the door, and I'm alone. I vaguely remember Jaeger getting up early, kissing my hair, and telling me he'd be back.

My hair is damp from a shower. Jaeger must have

cleaned me before tucking us into bed. I frown at my bare feet, remembering how I'd run from him over the cold stone. How I'd panicked in that dark, evil place, the horror growing in my belly until it had come clawing out and consumed me. My sex is raw, and my back is bruised from how hard he fucked me against the mausoleum wall.

More memories from last night come flooding in, and I sort through the shadowy fragments. The church that is not a church, the ritual that resulted in a man's murder, and a woman like me covered in blood. The demons in skull masks, the flames licking up the black walls like hellfire

It feels like a nightmare come to haunt me. Maybe I'll be lucky, and it'll all turn out to be a dream.

I don't think I'm that lucky.

My limbs feel like lead as I propel myself off the bed. My ankle isn't fully healed, but I'm able to limp to the bathroom and face the mirror.

There's still a ribbon around my neck, but it's not white. It's black.

Last night wasn't a dream.

What did I get myself into? I wish Jaeger was here so he could hold me and tell me it's all right. So I can cry and smack him until he pins me down and calls me bunny. He makes things make sense.

He's part of the darkness, but he's still my safe place.

I'm buttoning up my jeans, almost dressed and ready for the day, when the front door slams.

Jaeger must be back.

I limp out of the bedroom only to stop short. The man in the foyer is in ripped jeans and a black T-shirt, with long golden hair tied back from his face. He looks like Jaeger, but he's not.

It's Kaiser, prowling into the penthouse like he owns it.

I freeze like a rabbit sighted by the wolf.

He stops to sneer at the ferns and throw pillows but quickly transfers all his disgust into a glare directed at me.

I want to tell him to fuck off, but I don't want to die today. My only hope is that Jaeger comes back and throws him out.

Kaiser seems content to glare at me in silence. Maybe he's not here to kill me. Jaeger said Kaiser had an apartment nearby, right? So he's our neighbor. Maybe he's here to borrow an egg.

To break the awkwardness, I ask, "Can I help you?"

His glower turns darker, but finally, he speaks. "Do you know where my brother is right now?"

JAEGER

THIS MORNING, I woke up to a text consisting of only one word: *Inferno*. It was sent by Damien, who is listed in my phone only as the number one. Damien has always had enemies, and as Fraternitas grows in power and wealth, he's only made more. That's why he encourages the mystique surrounding the figure called "the Devil." The less he seems human and real, the safer he is.

Before he claimed his *elita*, he didn't care about his own safety. But now, he has more to live for.

I understand his way of thinking now that I have Elodie. I have more to worry about, more reason to care for my own life.

I can only hope Damien will forgive me for what I've done.

I left Elodie in our bed, still sleeping, worn out from our night together.

I'm lucky Damien called to meet him at Inferno rather than the underground. Those who are invited to the Abyss by the Devil do not return.

I find Damien in Lucy's office with her, their heads close together. The door is open, but they stop talking when I approach and rap the door frame out of courtesy.

Lucy looks me up and down and scoffs. "I'll talk to you later," she tells Damien and rolls her wheelchair out from behind her desk.

"Good to see you, Lucy," I tell her, and she waves her hand at me. She likes me, and being rude is her favorite way to show it.

Either that or she's worried about me. I broke a law last night.

To his credit, Damien does not waste time dancing around the subject. He stands and leans against the desk, waiting until I've shut the door to speak.

"I'm told you brought an uninitiated to church." He folds his arms across his chest.

I raise my arms and grin. "Guilty."

Damien fixes me with a glare. He's not as tall as me or as broad, but he's a savage fighter who's proven himself. Since we were children, he's been our leader. Father Francis was our patriarch and guide, but Damien was one of us. That's why he has the crown.

"The only reason I haven't thrown you to the Torturer in the Abyss is because St. James told me to give you a chance to say your piece. And I know you're loyal."

"I am. I was at your wedding when you claimed your reluctant bride."

It's dangerous to bring up The Devil's *elita*. He's crazy

about her, and claiming her has only made him more psychotically protective.

He rubs his chin and covers his mouth, masking his expression with the skull tattoo on the back of his hand. But he lets me speak.

"Did you know, when you first met her, that she'd be yours?"

He lets his hand slide down enough to answer. "Yes."

I lean against the wall, staring at the ceiling to find the words. "It's the same for me. You know my history. My past. The childhood I never had. I had nothing."

"None of us did."

"But I had my brother. We had each other, and then we had you. You made something of us. You and Father Francis and St. James. Together, we became something great. *Totum maius est partibus suis.*"

Damien's cheek quirks with a hint of a smile at my clumsy Latin.

"I'm grateful. I never wanted anything more." I pause to let this sink in. "Until her."

He sighs and says, "St. James said he gave you a reward."

"I've been fighting for so long. But now I want someone to fight for. To live for." I stop talking and wait. It's up to the Devil whether I live or die for my trespasses. But if I can't have Elodie, I don't want to live.

Damien lets out a heavy sigh. He rubs his hand over his face and then drops it to study his ring. "I understand."

Damien knows I would die for him and for my brothers. He'd do the same for me, for us. That's what it means to be Fraternitas.

And when we claim an *elita*, we make new vows. Damien would die for his chosen one, and so would I. My loyalty to Fraternitas extends to the one he's claimed. That's why we take care when we choose the one we'll claim. The *elita* ritual is more binding than a legal marriage. It's a vow written in blood.

"I need someone to cherish." There's an ache in my chest, deeper than any physical pain, as I think of my bunny waiting for me in my bed. "Elodie is that someone."

Damien is twisting and turning his Fraternitas ring. I know he's thinking of his *elita* and the long, hard road he took to claim her. "Then take her. With my blessing."

Eloldie is as good as mine.

I just have to convince her.

I turn to go.

"But Jaeger," Damien calls before I can open the door. I halt with my hand on the doorknob. "The rules say she must pass the test and prove her loyalty to Fraternitas. If not..."

If not, my life is at stake. I knew this when I brought her to the Abyss. "She'll pass the test." I'll make sure of it.

Or die trying.

∼

ELODIE

I STARE AT KAISER, who's glaring at me. I should be used to it by now, but he's scary up close.

"No. Should I?" I want to add that Jaeger does whatever he wants, but I don't want to mouth off too much to a man who hates me for no reason.

"This morning, he was summoned to speak with Damien. The one called the Devil? Do you know what that means?"

I want to say, *No, I don't know anything about your stupid brotherhood or its hierarchies.* Instead, I shake my head.

"It means they know. All of them. They know you were there."

He's talking about last night. The murder I'd witnessed. The ritual that binds Sarah to Fraternitas forever, and me as well.

Kaiser moves into the penthouse, heading toward the far wall. He opens the panel with the safe. I don't ask how he knows it's there or how he knows the code, but he unlocks it and holds up the briefcase with my cash.

"This is what you're going to do." He comes toward me, and I lock my legs to keep from backing away. "You're going to take this, and you're going to leave."

"What?"

"Get your purse," he orders. His voice is a quiet menace, and I don't dare disobey. I go back into the bedroom and return wearing shoes and a coat, purse in hand.

He opens the briefcase and motions me forward. "Take your money."

Without a word, I stuff as many stacks of bills as I can into my purse while Kaiser paces behind me.

"Now go."

I head to the foyer, where he's set a pair of crutches. He follows me all the way there, barely waiting for me to balance on the crutches before herding me out the door.

I stall in the hallway, a sob hitching in my throat. Does it end like this? Me leaving without a goodbye? Without a note?

It's what I'd planned to do all along... before I realized I was in love with Jaeger. Before I realized how much I needed a man like him. Someone who would fight for me. Someone who wouldn't leave and wouldn't let me leave.

But maybe it's for the best. I don't know if I'm strong enough to be with him, and he deserves someone who can enter his dark world with her head high.

Kaiser stands guard at his brother's door. He points toward the back elevator and folds his arms over his chest, making it clear he won't let me back in. He's going to watch me leave, and if I don't go, I'm sure I won't like what he does next.

I scramble away on my crutches, my bag banging around my legs. It's not until I'm outside, the sharp wind blowing in my face, that it hits me that I'm alone. All the fears and worries I had before meeting Jaeger bombard me like they've just been waiting for this moment. The moment I have no one. No more Jaeger to fix things with his fists or his money. He did more than let me lean on him. He carried me.

I'll never have that again. I'll never see him again. The thought crushes me.

I brush away frozen tears and try to think. I'm a survivor, right? I can figure this out.

But without Jaeger, there's not going to be much more to my life than surviving.

First things first. I need a ride that can't be traced to a hiding place that's far from here.

I go as far as I can on crutches until the nice buildings and shops give way to warehouses and shady-looking businesses. Then I duck into an alley, out of the wind.

I pull my phone from my coat pocket and scroll through my contacts. *Honey, Daria, Angel*—my friends from Inferno. I can't call them. They work for a business owned by Fraternitas, and I can't put them at risk.

When word gets out that I know what I know and that I've run, the brotherhood will hunt me down. It won't matter that Kaiser made me leave; they can't have someone out in the world who knows their secrets. They'll drag me to their murder-chapel and get rid of me. Jaeger won't be able to protect me.

He's not even here.

My thumb halts my scrolling on the name *Tommy*. He's one of my Narcotics Anonymous contacts, who texted me a few days ago, asking if I was going to a meeting anytime soon. Maybe he'll give me a ride.

He answers on the third ring. "Elodie?"

"Hey," I say, and my voice cracks. It's hitting me, what I'm doing. How I'm leaving Jaeger. I won't ever see him again.

Or he'll catch me, and I'll be dead.

I force myself to ask Tommy for a favor, a ride. "I know it's weird, but can you come pick me up?"

He seems surprised but says he can come. I thank him and give him the cross streets, hang up, and press myself against the brick wall to wait.

This is the start of my new life. No more Jaeger. No more late-night fucks or cuddles or confessions in the dark. No one to growl at me in their deep voice and call me "Bunny."

No more rom-coms on the couch.

Just me, on the run, forever. Praying that my family will stay safe, and that I can stay one step ahead of the hunters.

It's enough to make me want to crumple into a ball on the concrete.

The wind shifts, whistling between the buildings with enough force to steal my breath. It's freezing, but I lean into it. If I'm lucky, it'll numb me so I don't feel the pain cracking open my chest anymore.

Eventually, Tommy comes. But he's not alone.

15

E lodie

TOMMY'S tiny white beater pulls up to the alleyway. The cold has made my limbs stiff, but I shift to standing and greet him. He gets out, shading his face from the wind. "Elodie?"

Before I can swing on my crutches over to him, another car, one I don't recognize, pulls up. It's long, low, black, and expensive.

My heart stutters in my chest. Did Fraternitas find me so quickly?

The men who get out of the second car aren't wearing skull rings, but they do look like thugs, though.

One of them holds the door open as a man in a suit climbs out and scowls at the wind, buttoning up his wool overcoat.

"I'm sorry," Tommy mouths to me, and my heart sinks to my feet.

Oh, Tommy, what have you done?

"This her?" the suit asks Tommy.

"Yeah." Tommy doesn't look at me. He scuffs the pavement with his sneaker.

This was why Tommy texted me out of the blue. It's a trap, and I'm the stupid bunny who hopped right into it.

I move to the middle of the alley, but the thugs are already closing in.

"Get outta here," one of them orders Tommy, and my friend gets back in his car and does as he's told. My heart sinks, watching Tommy drive away.

"Hello, Elodie. I've been looking everywhere for you." The suit smiles, and a gold tooth flashes at me. "Umberto sends his regards."

Umberto, the loan shark, who's been after Margot and me.

Adrenaline screams through me, telling me to run, but the thugs have me surrounded. "I have money," I croak.

"That's good. That'll help. But I want something more. Tommy tells me you have an in with Fraternitas."

I almost laugh out loud. My life is ending, and everything's surreal.

I shake my head.

"Don't lie to me, Elodie. I don't like it. He said he's seen you with one of them. And these guys, they get possessive. Apparently this guy was all over you. Intimate-like." His tone of voice makes me want to scrub out my ears with bleach.

"That was then," I say. "It's not like that anymore. But I can give you cash. For the loan. It's in here." I hold up my purse.

One of the thugs comes and takes the whole thing out of

my hands. I keep quiet. It'll suck, but if I'm lucky, I can trade the contents for my life.

The thug fishes in my bag and holds up a wad of cash. The suit's eyes narrow.

"You've been holding out on me." The thug paws through my bag, taking a quick count. He recites a number to the suit, who says, "I guess being a Fraternitas mistress pays."

I wasn't his mistress. I was more than that. I hear Jaeger saying, *I love you, and you love me, too*, and the thought warms me, even though I've left him behind.

"Take the money. All of it," I say. "Just let me go."

"We could do that. Or we could take you, too, and trade you for millions." Ice slides down my spine. This is what I was afraid of. "All those Fraternitas guys are loaded."

"He won't pay for me. He kicked me to the curb. Do I look like I'm with him?" I spread my hands.

"Except you're wearing that ribbon around your neck."

I touch my throat, and he's right. I forgot to remove it. One night wearing it, and it's already a part of me. I could tear it off, but it's too late. These guys have seen it, and I want to keep any remaining memento of Jaeger I can get.

And it doesn't matter because the suit says, "He's already put the word out that you belong to him."

"Like I said, that was then. Things change. "The wind blows my hair into my mouth, but I speak through it. "Men leave, all of them." Even as I say it, I know it's a lie.

Jaeger would never leave me.

You belong to me. And in his world, a vow like that cuts both ways. I was his, but he was mine, too. He chose me. And no matter what happens, he'll always be the one for me.

As if I've conjured him out of my head, Jaeger's voice echoes down the alleyway. "Elodie."

I close my eyes, hoping I've imagined it. But no.

Jaeger stands at the mouth of the alley. He's in jeans and his black leather jacket. No weapons that I can see. But he doesn't need any.

He prowls closer.

"Stop right there," one of the thugs says.

Jaeger doesn't stop coming toward me. "I heard you wanted to speak to me," he says without taking his eyes from mine. I sink into their ocean depths.

Did he hear what the thugs said? How long has he been here?

"Do you have business with my Elodie?" he asks the suit.

"Matter of fact, we did. But now we'd like to talk to you."

"So talk."

"I've heard of you and your brother." The suit sounds like a fanboy. "You were legends in the fighting rings. And you were what, seventeen?"

"Fifteen. We were made to fight." Jaeger stops a few feet away and holds out a hand to me. "Elodie, come here."

It takes a moment for the signal to go from my brain to my legs, but I go to him. The distance is a hundred thousand miles, but it takes no time at all.

"Jaeger," I whisper because he's here, and he's running his eyes over me, looking for signs that I've been hurt. He touches his thumb to my lips, and warmth returns to my body.

But I'm breathing again. My heart's beating. And I realize that, since leaving the penthouse, I've felt like I died.

"You killed your trainer." The suit is still yapping.

"He wasn't our trainer. He was our handler. And yes, we killed him. But back to the matter at hand." Jaeger grips my shoulder and turns to the suit. "You were saying something about a trade?"

The suit signals, and the thugs close around us. "I think we can come to an agreement. Just give us what we want, and we'll go. Ten million."

"You know who I am."

"They call you the Wolf." The suit shifts from foot to foot. Maybe he's realizing how dumb it is to shakedown a member of Fraternitas. "You can't take all of us."

Jaeger raises a brow. "Are you prepared to wager your life on that?"

In answer, one of the thugs draws his gun.

"All right," Jaeger says. "You win." He smiles, and all the thugs take a step back, even the one holding the gun.

Jaeger presses a phone against my chest and slips it into my inner pocket. "Do not stop until you are safe. Call my brother; he will pick you up."

"Jaeger, I—" I don't know what I want to say. *I'm sorry. I'm glad you're here. Don't do this.*

"Go." He pushes me.

"Not so fast," the suit says.

"Let her go." Jaeger lifts his arms. "You want me. I'll give you the money if you can knock me out. All of you against one of me. Should be easy."

"You're not armed?" the thug closest to him asks.

"Not with a gun."

Everyone's frozen, staring at Jaeger. "What are you waiting for?" Jaeger taunts. "Come take me."

One of the thugs makes a move toward me, but Jaeger snarls, "Touch her and die," and the thug stops.

I hustle away, getting into a swinging rhythm with the crutches to take me toward the street.

I don't want to see the violence that's about to unfold.

At least that's what I tell myself.

But at the end of the alley, I hesitate. The wind sends crumbled food wrappers and newspapers tumbling past my feet.

I could go now. Toss Jaeger's phone and really run away. Leave him. I imagined this moment and the path to escape laid out before me. Now that it's here, it's clear to me that I would never choose to run.

I choose Jaeger. I'll always choose him.

I'd rather die in an alley with him than run and live. Because a life without him is no life at all.

I pull out his phone. It's locked, but after a moment's hesitation, I enter the date we met, and it unlocks.

The last number called is to someone named K. I guess that's Kaiser. I hit redial, and before the first ring, he picks up and grunts, "What?"

"Alley off Daphne Street." I glance up at the street signs. "Near the shut down spice factory. Ten, maybe eleven men. They've cornered Jaeger."

I don't wait for him to ask questions. I pocket the phone and whirl.

The thugs are circling Jaeger. What is their stupid plan anyway? Make him withdraw money from an ATM? They're nuts if they think Fraternitas will allow them to live long.

So these are desperate men. Desperate and stupid. Not a great combination.

How is Jaeger going to get out of this?

The thugs surround Jaeger, and the suit draws a gun.

"Jaeger!" I scream. His head whips around, and I point to the suited thug. "Look out!"

Two of the thugs dart in to grab him. He tussles, but they grab his arms and hold him.

The suit raises the gun and takes aim.

"No!" I shriek and torpedo forward. I'm not armed. The only thing I have are my crutches, so I swing one upward and hurl it with all my might.

~

JAEGER

THE THUGS ARE close enough that I can smell their bad breath. I peer beyond the men to see Elodie reach the end of the alley and raise my cell to make a call.

Soon, she'll be safe. That's all that matters.

The suit is droning on about his plan to get us to take a nice, quiet ride across the river so I can transfer money from my bank to Umberto's. I make note of the name. He's just moved to the top of my own list of People I Want to Kill, right after these goons.

There's a shriek and a blur of motion. Elodie screams for me to look out.

Two thugs grab me, and I'm too focused on Elodie to care that the suit has brought out a gun.

"No!" Elodie cries.

A crutch goes flying through the air and hits the suit in the face.

There's a blast, and a bullet ricochets off the brick wall behind Elodie.

And the beast breaks free. Rage pumps through my bloodstream. The world goes still, covered in a red haze.

I have to protect my woman. She needs me.

I wrench my arms, pulling the men who hold me. They fall off balance, and I crack their heads together. They go down for good, and I leap over them, heading for the suit.

He's turned toward Elodie, and now she's facing down a gun barrel. The blood has drained from her face, leaving her freckles stark on her pale cheeks. The man is saying something. Threatening her.

It'll be his last mistake.

I hit him like a linebacker, and we crash to the ground. His head strikes the pavement. So does his gun hand. The weapon goes skidding away.

I slam the man's head into the ground again and again. Blood spatters on my face, but I don't stop until he's dead.

Elodie's nearby, huddled against the wall. Once he's taken care of, I race to get between her and the rest of the thugs.

More men come to tackle me like I tackled their leader. I dodge them, then attack them one by one. Break their bones. Crack their skulls. Let their brains ooze out like overripe fruit.

A crack of a bullet. Something bites at my side.

Damn, I forgot to secure the gun. There are no weapons in the fighting ring. I forgot where I was.

I whirl around, and pain lances my side. But I can deal with the pain.

Something clatters at my feet. A wooden crutch. I snatch it up and use it like a club to beat down the man with the gun. He tries to shoot me again, but he's not fast enough. His blood paints the sidewalk.

I stagger back, feeling light-headed. Blood loss. I remember this feeling from my time in the ring. I hit the wall and let it support me as I slide down to the ground.

The alley is full of the crumpled shapes of my victims. Good.

Elodie's screaming.

Bunny, no. It'll be okay. I'm bleeding out, but I want to reassure her.

She's on her knees beside me. Her freckles are stark on her tear-streaked face.

I love her freckles so much.

She grabs my hand.

"You came back for me." I squeeze her fingers. My own fingers are stiff and cold.

"Jaeger, oh gods—"

"Are you hurt?"

"You're shot!" She's shaking.

I pull her down so her face is close to mine. I want to kiss her.

She won't let me. "You're bleeding,"

"It's nothing."

She opens my leather jacket and turns ghostly pale. "I have to stop the bleeding." She pulls her scarf off, wads it up, and presses it to my midriff.

"We should leave." Even my lips feel cold. "Before the pigs come." The alley's littered with bodies, and there's a red river running in the valley between the dumpsters. The police won't like that. St. James and Lucy have the cops in their pocket, but they'll bitch about the paperwork.

"Shut up."

A shadow falls over us both, and she flinches. I start struggling to sit up until I see it's Kaiser.

Finally.

～

ELODIE

. . .

Blood. There's so much blood, and Jaeger's cheeks have lost their color.

Then someone's growling, "What the hell?" above my head. I bite back a scream and look up to see Kaiser. I didn't even hear him approach.

"He's shot," I snap. "You've got to help him."

"I'm here." Atticus appears and pushes me aside. I scramble out of the way so he can open his medical case and go to work.

"What happened?" Kaiser glowers at me, but I've had it.

"What happened is you kicked me out, and then my friend sold me out to a bunch of idiots." I can't believe I'm yelling at the scary twin. "Jaeger tried to save me, and he got shot."

Kaiser reaches for me, and I lose it. I push at his solid chest, shrieking, "This is all your fault!"

Kaiser growls, and I brace for retaliation. I'm so mad I don't care.

"Will you two stop? We need to get out of here."

We both whirl to see Atticus helping Jaeger to his feet.

"But," I start. Jaeger looks half unconscious. There's a bandage wrapped tightly around his middle, but a red stain is rapidly blooming.

"I got him stable. Let's go."

There's a car at the end of the alleyway that Atticus steers Jaeger toward. Kaiser moves to support his other side.

I limp after them, leaning on one crutch. I go as fast as I can, but I'm still the last to arrive. Atticus rides with Jaeger in the backseat, and I fall into the passenger seat just as Kaiser is starting the car.

"Where are your crutches?" Kaiser glares at me.

"She threw it at the man with the gun." Jaeger has a goofy grin on his face.

Kaiser raises a brow.

"It didn't work," I mutter. "It just made him mad."

"It distracted him." Jaeger lifts his hand and examines the blood dripping off it. To my shock, he opens his mouth as if he's going to lick it off his fingers.

"No." Atticus smacks his hand. "Unsanitary. Bloodborne pathogens. Disease." Jaeger snarls at him, showing his teeth, and Atticus shakes his head. "Kaiser, you tell him."

"Brother." Blue eyes meet blue eyes in the rearview mirror. "You did it. Your woman saved you, and you saved her. Now you heal so you can protect her another day."

"So you agree? She is my woman?"

"She is."

"I'm right here," I snip because they're talking over me. My heart is pounding so hard it's painful in my chest. I cross my arms to hide my shaking hands.

"She's grouchy when she's afraid," Jaeger informs the car.

"Ah," Kaiser puts the car into gear, and the tires squeal as he guns it down the street.

"I'm here, bunny," Jaeger tells me. "And I'll live. It's just a little bullet. You can nurse me back to health."

"You'll have to use crutches." I tighten my arms around my torso as if they can hold me together. "Don't expect me to carry you everywhere."

JAEGER

I WAS LUCKY. The bullet got me in the gut, but Atticus got me into surgery in time. As soon as he could, St. James invested in a hospital. There's a whole wing dedicated to Fraternitas, furnished with the best medical equipment and staffed by a team of discreet nurses.

I come awake with Elodie sitting to my left. She's folded in half, resting on my bed.

There's an IV in my right arm and a dull ache in my abs.

I reach out and stroke Elodie's curls, and she raises her head. Her eyes are huge and dark on her pale face.

I try to tell her it's okay, and my voice comes out a dull rasp.

She scrambles to get me a cup of water to sip from. I drink, holding her gaze until I can speak clearly.

"It's okay, bunny."

She sniffles.

"No, don't cry." I can't bear to see her dark eyes fill with tears. "I'm here, and we're together, so I'm okay."

Her voice hitches as she says, "You came for me."

"Of course. You're my woman."

Her sob shudders out of her.

"You can run from me, but I'll chase you, and I will find you. I will always find you."

Her bottom lip trembles and it breaks my heart. I reach up to swipe some of the tears off her face.

"You were my birthday present. The only one I've ever had."

"I know." She mouths, turning her face into my hand. I wait until her tears have stopped and wipe them away with my palm.

"Will you wait for me?"

"What?"

"Will you wait to run again until I'm healed? So I can chase you?"

"Yes." Her face crumbles, and her voice cracks, but she says, "I'll wait."

"Good bunny." I smile and let myself drift off.

When I wake again, Elodie's asleep, clutching my hand. There's a shadowy figure in the corner and another hovering in the door.

Damien says, "I heard you were shot. Atticus says you won't die."

I lean my head back so I can look at him. "Not today."

He nods and leaves. Kaiser lingers in the doorway for a moment. "I'm sorry, brother."

I narrow my eyes at him. I slowly move the hand connected to the IV and place it on Elodie's head.

"I nearly got you both killed. I'll never forgive myself."

"I'm hard to kill. But you made my woman cry."

"I didn't know those goons were after her." He swears at himself. "I should've known."

"I don't give a fuck," I rasp. The anger I felt when I came home and learned what he did was still there. At the time, I had been focused on hunting Elodie down with the tracker I had on her phone.

And now she's beside me, unhurt. Kaiser and I are brothers, but Elodie comes first. I won't forgive him unless she does.

I tell him that, and he says, "I'll make it up to you."

"To her," I correct, and he sighs. But then he nods. He shuts the door, but if I know him, he'll keep watch outside our door. He'll stay there, guarding us all night.

It's not enough to forgive him for trying to separate me and my woman, but it's a start.

The following day, I make them move me back home. Elodie fusses, but Atticus allows it. I'm healing just fine, and

I'll sleep better in my own bed with Elodie curled next to me.

It all goes smoothly until Kaiser insists on staying to guard me. Elodie doesn't like it.

"You're on her People She Wants to Kill List," I tell Kaiser. The painkillers Atticus has me on make me talk.

"Really?" Kaiser gives Elodie a look.

She sucks in a breath. She's still afraid of him, a little bit.

"He won't hurt you," I tell Elodie. "Ever again. I'll kill him if he does."

They both eye each other warily, but now everything's out in the open. It might be the drugs talking, but I feel good. This is progress.

I sit on the couch with Elodie cuddled close. Kaiser takes a lounge chair and scowls at the TV.

"What is this shit?" He points to the screen, where a hardworking CEO has come back home to the small town of Hollydale to save her family's Christmas inn.

Elodie tenses. "It's a movie."

Kaiser speaks over her head to me. "There's a game on." He reaches for the remote.

"No," Elodie growls.

"I want to watch this," I say, so they won't fight. On-screen, the heroine's childhood sweetheart shows up just in time to save her when she slips on a patch of ice. They stand up under some hanging mistletoe.

Kaiser mutters under his breath but keeps watching.

Ten minutes later, when the heroine's fiancé shows up to drag her back to the big city: "He's a tool. She can do better."

Elodie's eyes go wide, but I give her a squeeze and say, "I agree. Never trust a guy in a black turtleneck sweater."

Elodie slips out of my grasp. "I'm getting popcorn."

Twenty minutes later, Kaiser leans forward, crunching a

giant handful of popcorn. "This is stupid," he says, eyes fixed on the screen. "She's not in love with him."

"She has to go back. Someone has to run her company," Elodie argues, her eyes twinkling.

"It wasn't making her happy. She should just stay, marry the handyman, and run the inn."

I fall asleep, listening to my two favorite people in the world bicker about a silly movie. This is my life now. My family. Everything I longed for as a child but never thought I could have. All it took was the love of a woman brave enough to stay by my side.

Later, when I wake up, they're watching the movie with the widow and the long-lost prince.

ELODIE

THE FIRST NIGHT back at home, I feel like I should give Jaeger space by sleeping on the couch, but he insists I stay next to him in the bed. He wakes when I try to slip away.

"No." He grabs my wrist and pulls me close.

I resist, keeping my distance so I don't jostle him. "Jaeger, you were shot."

"I'm not dead." He's still strong enough to muscle me down, although I give in quickly because I don't want him to open his wounds. But then he sets my hand on his crotch.

"Oh my gods," I mutter because he's hard as a rock.

"You can nurse me back to health."

I protest, but he pushes down his sweatpants and fists his hands in my hair, guiding me down. "Suck me."

I nuzzle his cock, taking in his salty scent. I'll never tell him, but it's reassuring to have him manhandle me like this. Every time he tugs my hair, I get wet. "This can't be good for you."

"Atticus approved. I already asked."

"Of course you did." I roll my eyes and open my mouth for him. I try to do most of the work, but he bucks his hips, filling me with his taste and scent. He doesn't force himself down my throat, but he guides my head in the proper rhythm until his cock swells.

"Swallow," he orders, and I do. I lick my lips and let him pull me back up so he can kiss me.

He rests a hand around my throat. I've kept the black ribbon tied where he put it. "Soon, this will be a collar," he says.

I swallow, my throat muscles working against his palm, but I don't deny it. I've chosen Jaeger, and now he chooses for me. It's blissful, this surrender.

He slips his free hand between my legs and starts to toy with me. He can feel how wet I am. "You'll like it. You like being my woman."

He waits for me to answer, and when I don't, he stops touching me until I say, "Yes."

"Good bunny." His fingers tighten around my throat, and I only get wetter. I shut my eyes and let him tease me higher. "As soon as I'm healed, I'll claim you."

I suck in a breath, and he rubs me harder. "You don't need to worry. Give all that to me. You don't have to shoulder it anymore. You'll let me lead." I squirm, but he's got me pinned between the hand at my throat and the fingers in my cunt. My world narrows to those two points.

"You will be my chosen." His breath warms my cheek. "I can't wait to see you on your knees, in front of my brothers, accepting my collar." His cruel fingers twist inside me, and I whimper. "That's what you want, isn't it? To be safe. To be mine forever."

My sex tightens under his touch, and I spiral higher. I reach for him, needing something to hold onto. This violent, dangerous man is my safe space. I slip my hand under his shirt, and my fingers find the rough edges of his brand, the skull burned into his back. For some reason, the long-healed scar soothes me.

"Don't worry, bunny. No one touches you. Nobody but me."

"Jaeger," I pant. I can barely think, but I have to say this. "I need you."

He smiles and rubs me faster.

"Oh gods, I need it."

"I know, bunny. I'll give you everything." He kisses me so sweetly. "Just give yourself to me. You'll have to pass a test, but you can do it." He finds the spot that makes my body light up, and I'm so far gone I can't even feel fear.

What would you do if you were not afraid?

"It'll be okay. I'll be with you every step of the way."

My climax breaks, and I let it wash me away. Jaeger keeps hold of my neck as he kisses me and whispers, "You belong to the Big Bad Wolf."

16

E *lodie*

JAEGER and I are cuddling on the couch when the front door opens. Kaiser walks in, as he always does, like he owns the place. He almost knocks over one of the orchids, and I hear him cussing at it. He acts like he hates our penthouse decor, but I overheard him asking Jaeger where he could buy 'shit like these little pillows.'

I pause the rom-com we're watching. "You have a visitor," I say to Jaeger. I sound surly.

"Actually, I'm here for you." Instead of heading into the kitchen to forage in our fridge, like he usually does, Kaiser comes straight over to us. He's holding a pair of crutches. "Jaeger says he will forgive me if you do."

"Okay." My voice is tight.

"You make my brother happy. He deserves happiness."

He hands me the crutches. "For you. A gift." They have a big red bow on them and everything.

"You already gave me crutches." Right before he threw me out. Is he going to try to do that again?

"These are special. Watch." He picks one up and holds it between us. "Touch the hidden trigger, and—" A blade shoots out of the bottom with a *snick*.

I slam myself back against the couch cushions.

Jaeger chuckles. "Let me see." He takes the crutches and shows me how to trigger the blade.

"For protection," Kaiser tells me.

"You can keep me safe," Jaeger jokes.

I look from brother to brother, my mouth open. "I'm not... I don't need murder crutches."

Kaiser raises his brows.

"We'll practice with them." Jaeger takes the crutches and sets them close to me.

Oh gods.

"And she'll forgive you. One day." Jaeger swipes his thumb over my cheek, and I growl.

"Good." Kaiser glances at the TV and heads to the kitchen to get the popcorn. I've already half-forgiven the idiot. He's a thug and a surly asshole, but it's easy to understand why when I think of him as a kid. Kaiser's fiercely protective of his brother and has resented me for taking up space in Jaeger's life. He hadn't wanted to share.

The twins are still emotionally stunted, but their taste in holiday rom-coms gives me hope.

"You're still high on the list of People She Wants to Kill," Jaeger informs him. "But so am I."

"I can live with it if you can." Kaiser settles into his chair and grabs the remote. He unpauses the movie, and I pretend to watch while the brothers keep murmuring to each other.

"We're not at the top, though," Jaeger says. "Of the list."

"Oh? Who's number one?"

I could cover my ears, but I don't, so I hear when Jaeger says, "A man from her past. But he won't hold the spot for long."

~

JAEGER

MY GUNSHOT WOUND gives us a month to prepare for the claiming ritual. It also gives Kaiser time to track down a certain member from her past and lay the groundwork for his disappearance. Fraternitas is powerful, but when it comes to prominent members of society, it's best to obscure our connection to their death. It'll be safer for Elodie.

Ten days before the big night, I start edging her. She pouts and sighs but lets me touch her carefully and slowly and stop before she goes over. I lay my hand on her quivering belly and listen to her fight to control her breathing.

The night of her collaring, Elodie gets a visitor. Kaiser opens the door, and Lucy rolls in. Her usual glower softens when she sees my penthouse.

"Jaeger, love what you've done with the place." The tattoo vines on her arms ripple as she wheels around, giving herself a tour.

Elodie uses one of her new crutches to rise and greet her boss. She looks surprised to see Lucy and blanches when she sees Lucy's right hand.

Lucy notices her reaction. "Oh yes." She holds up her hand, showing off the skull ring. There's a black pearl in one of the eye sockets. "I have one of these, too. I don't wear it in public. No need to broadcast my status to civilians."

"Lucy's one of the Seven," I tell Elodie. Her eyes widen further.

"Another thing I don't advertise. Jaeger, is there somewhere Elodie and I can talk in private?"

They end up in my bedroom. I take Elodie's second crutch and lean on it while I lurk outside the door, eavesdropping.

Lucy doesn't waste time on small talk. "Do you know what happens tonight?"

"Yes." Elodie's voice is soft, muffled by the door.

"And you understand the rules?"

"Loyalty to Fraternitas or death," Elodie recites what I've taught her.

Lucy's voice lowers. "Are you sure about this?"

"Yes." Elodie clears her throat and repeats louder, "Yes."

There's a long pause, and Lucy says, "I gave your friends the rest of the afternoon and night off. They'll be at Club Empire. But not the ritual after. Understand?"

Elodie murmurs something, and then the door opens, and Lucy comes out. She sees me and snorts, wheeling close enough to nearly run over my toe.

"So glad you could visit," I tell her. "Come again."

"I will." She pauses halfway to the door, taking a gander at the TV. "Is this the one with the lumberjack who saves Christmas?"

I nod, hiding my surprise that Lucy knows the plot of a rom-com.

"Kaiser told me it was good. Maybe I'll come watch one with you sometime."

I leave Lucy to let herself out and go to Elodie.

She's sitting on the bed. Her hand is at her throat,

absently playing with the ribbon there. I don't even know if she's aware she's doing it. I sit and take her hands in mine, then push her to her back.

She goes willingly. She's used to me maneuvering her to a prone position so I can edge her.

I flip up her sweater dress and inspect the gusset of her panties. They're damp but not soaking. Not yet.

Elodie sucks in a breath when I very lightly run my thumb up and down her inner thigh. "You spoke to Lucy about tonight."

"You were listening, weren't you?"

I don't bother to deny it. "You said you were sure about the ritual."

"I better be."

I stop touching her until she explains, "I've found that in life, one choice flows from another."

"And that means?"

"It means I'm sure about you. And that makes me sure about the rest."

The front door bangs open, and Elodie jumps. I press my palm to her sex, grounding her before flipping her dress back down and helping her up. "Your friends are here. They'll get you ready."

Elodie

Honey, Daria, and Angel all come and help me prepare. I hear them enter the penthouse, and their loud voices ring out, and then fall to a hush when Kaiser greets them.

Jaeger opens the bedroom door for them, and they all troop in. Once he shuts the door, they get loud again.

"We got the night off," Honey cries happily. "Lucy said so."

"She told me," I say. "She was just here."

"Lucy was here?" Daria looks around, wide-eyed like Lucy might magically appear.

"You're so obsessed with her." Angel gives her a playful push.

"Shut up, I am not," Daria says so vehemently that I raise my brows. I make a note to study her interactions with Lucy next time I'm at Inferno.

Honey sets up her makeup case and starts prepping my skin while peppering me with questions. "Was that Jaeger's brother at the door?"

"Yes. He's always hanging around now."

"Doesn't he hate you?"

"He's come around."

Daria plops down on the bed next to me with enough force that Honey scolds her. Angel pulls out a bag of dark chocolate.

"So. Tonight. He's claiming you?"

"That's the plan." I ignore the little flutters in my gut. My nerves are eclipsed by the needy pulsing in my clit. All the work Jaeger put into edging me has seen to that.

I've kept my promise to him and haven't run. He's healing up faster than me, but I have crutches now. In theory, I could get away.

After tonight, it'll be too late. I'll be bound to him. I'll enter his world and let the darkness close over me.

Because of Jaeger, the shadows don't seem so scary anymore. He loves me, and I love him. I'm no longer prey to anyone but him, and that's only when we play our game.

With him, I have protection and a safe place to land.

With me, he has rom-coms on the couch. A home. Someone who cares for him and loves him as intensely as he loves me.

Angel had asked me what I'd do if I weren't afraid, and now I know.

I'm not afraid anymore.

The drive to the collaring ceremony goes by in a blur. Jaeger edges me to a frenzy in the car and leads me in with his fingers shackled around my wrist. He whispers that some *elita* ceremonies require the Fraternitas member to fuck his chosen in front of everyone. But he won't do that because he doesn't want anyone to see me naked. "No one but me."

My friends are allowed to come to the club to watch the first half of the ceremony, the part that's held at Club Empire. They don't understand everything about this dark world, but they're here to support me, and I love them for it.

Jaeger leads me out in front of the crowd and has me kneel. It's surreal, being in the center of the ceremony after watching one the night of Pandemonium. I feel small and vulnerable, surrounded by the tall, menacing members of Fraternitas. But I'm wet. My fear and arousal seem to go hand in hand.

Jaeger takes his place in front of me, and the flutters in my stomach calm. But my pussy throbs all the harder.

Beyond Jaeger, I catch a glimpse of my friends. Honey is wide-eyed, staring at the masked men. Daria has her arms crossed over her chest. Angel gives me a little wave.

And then St. James steps onto the platform with me and Jaeger, and I tense. *Run away!* A little voice screams in the back of my head. But it's too late.

As if he knows I'm freaking out, Jaeger reaches down and

cups the side of my neck. He lifts my head until I'm holding his gaze.

And the rest of the ceremony washes over me, with me staring into Jaeger's stormy eyes.

"Do you vow to love and honor your *elita?* Will you care for her and keep her, and cherish her above others? Will you fight to protect her, and put her safety before all else, even your own life?"

"I so vow." Jaeger holds my gaze. A jolt runs through me, and there's a great rushing sound in my ears, drowning out a few of St. James' next words. Jaeger explained that the vows are changed, depending on the willingness of the *elita.*

"And you, Elodie."

I startle when he says my name.

"Do you vow to submit to Jaeger, and wear his collar as a sign of your loyalty and love? Will you honor and obey him, and give yourself over to him in full and complete surrender?"

Jaeger warned me what was coming, but nothing could prepare me for how the ground feels like it's dropped away. Only Jaeger's gaze anchors me, keeps me from falling.

But I want him too much to turn back now. *Surrender.*

I say, on a shaky breath, "I do."

Jaeger leans in and seals it with a kiss.

A minute later, I'm wearing his collar. The white gold is a comforting weight around my neck and already feels like a part of me.

My friends approach and give me brief hugs, whispering congratulations before being ushered away. The collaring ceremony was only the first part of the night. The second part is only for members of Fraternitas.

Once again, I'm blindfolded and led to the underworld.

When the blindfold lifts, I'm standing in the vast sanctuary in front of a crowd of robed figures. The flames flicker in the walls, casting eerie shadows over the hooded faces of Fraternitas.

Lucy's here along with Father Francis and the leadership of Fraternitas. But I barely notice them because Jaeger's standing close to me.

I lean on one of the crutches Kaiser had given me and let the ritual wash over me.

The last time I was here, I didn't know what was going on. Now I do. Father Francis speaks the ritual in Latin, but Jaeger explained the vows to me earlier.

You vow loyalty to Fraternitas and all its members.

You vow to uphold the rule of the Devil and his Seven.

Above all, you commit your life to the one you have chosen. You will be bound together by water, by fire, by death, and by blood. So shall you vow.

"Yes, I so vow," Jaeger speaks first. After a pause, I echo it. I'm not as loud as him, but the cavernous chamber carries my voice to the back of the room.

A set of doors in the back slam open, and Kaiser and another masked executioner drag a man toward the ritual pool.

Heat flares through me, followed by a chill. I can feel my bare feet on the stone. It's warmer than I would expect, or maybe my body only thinks it's warm because of the flickering firelight.

And then I'm floating, and it feels like I'm watching everything unfold from up on the balcony. I look down on myself and note how calm I look for someone having an out-of-body experience.

"I'm here," Jaeger murmurs. He touches me, and I feel

his fingers on my elbow, but I'm still out of my body, looking down at the scene.

It's like watching something on a movie screen. The hooded figures, the frightening tableau. The cast surrounds the main actress, who has a wealth of red, curly hair and wears a white silk shift. She's barefoot with a collar around her neck and leaning on a crutch, waiting.

I watch her blanch when she recognizes the man the executioners drag forward. He's gagged and bound in a torn and dirty polo shirt and slacks, but she can imagine him standing in front of a college class, gesturing to a white-board. Or in his office, smugly telling her what she can do to earn a TA position that will allow her to stay in school. He rolled back in his chair and spread his legs—

And then I'm back in my body, facing the man who assaulted me. Who told me my grades depended on letting him do whatever he wanted to my body. Who preyed upon me until my stomach twisted, and I skipped classes to avoid him. And eventually, I dropped out. Even then, I couldn't escape the nightmares of him, so I retreated into pills.

He's here, on his knees before me, with two burly executioners gripping him to keep him still. And I have a choice. I didn't then, but I do now.

This world is full of people who do evil. Some are like Jaeger, who kills like a wolf. Quickly and without remorse. He wears a skull ring as proof of what he is.

But worse are the people who pretend to be good and use their position to prey on others. They hide their evil behind their reputation so no one believes their victims.

For much of my life, I've run from my problems. I've run from trouble. That's how I've survived.

I've spent my whole life as prey. I hated it, but I didn't know how to stop it. How else to survive.

All my life, I've had to take it. And I don't want to take it anymore.

Professor Boylin looks thinner and weaker than I remember him. Tied and gagged, a prisoner in the Abyss. One of the damned.

I'm the one who has sentenced him to die, and it was so easy. I'm doing it for the administration who didn't believe me. For my ex-boyfriend who laughed and said, "What do you expect? You're a hot piece of ass." For my friends who told me, "Professor Boylin would never. . ."

His blood will be on my hands.

I lift the crutch until the bottom of it is level with his eye. My arm wavers under the weight, but Jaeger is there, taking the base of the crutch and holding it steady so it's pressed against the prisoner's eye socket.

"I love you," he whispers to me.

I nod and pull the trigger. I don't need to watch the blade shoot out, driving deep through an eyeball into the brain.

I feel the recoil in my arm. There's little blood, but the body in front of me goes limp. It's no longer a person.

And I'm no longer prey. Tonight, I join the ranks of the predators.

And we will feast.

Jaeger leads me away from the body to the place where Lucy sits. We link hands over the silver dish, and she pours a cup of bloody water over our joined hands. Bathing us in blood, Lucy intones, "And now you are one."

I'm in a daze. I stare up at Jaeger, needing him to tell me what to do next.

He releases me, grips my hair, and kisses me. I relax, letting him take control. Reveling in it.

"You did it," he whispers against my mouth, and I push to tiptoe, leaning into him. Rubbing my hard nipples over his bare chest. He grunts, and I remember his bandages, his half-healed wound, but he doesn't let me back away.

So I fist my hands in his hair and kiss him back.

Because I'm like him now. His equal. I can run from him and let him chase me. I've learned that I like this when it's fake and play-acting. Choosing it makes me powerful. But I'm no longer the prey in my own life.

Kaiser and the others are removing the body. The man who preyed upon me is just a sack of meat. I didn't expect it to feel so good.

"What will happen to him?" I ask, and Lucy turns to answer me.

"There's an incinerator. We'll turn him to dust. Keep his teeth as trophies and scatter the rest of him to the wind." She gives me a feral smile. "Welcome to Fraternitas."

Jaeger puts his hand on my back, and I let him lead me away. We pass the ranks of robed members, and I hold my head high.

And then he's pushing me in front of him and telling me to run. My ankle twinges a little, but I dart ahead of him in the darkened hallway, wanting the thrill of running from a powerful hunter. I look back to make sure he's chasing me. He comes toward me, firelight licking across his face. His blue eyes are full of hunger.

I suck in a breath and whirl, racing away.

I don't get far.

He grabs me and pushes me down to my hands and knees. His hand is on the back of my neck, tugging on my collar.

He thrusts inside me, and I'm so hot for him it only takes a few thrusts before I cum. My cries echo through the corridor. He slams into me from behind, again and again, and I orgasm, this time hard enough to break in two. My fingers curl, and my nails break and chip on the black marble.

On the wall in front of me, our shadows tangle and merge. My palms are sore, and my knees are bruised by the time Jaeger grunts and spills into me. His cock pulses, and he scrapes his teeth over my bare shoulder. I shudder in pleasure.

His weight sags into me, and it feels so good. But the moment passes, and I grow uncomfortable being crushed.

I sit up and knock into him. He grunts, and I remember his gut wound.

"Did I hurt you?" I reach out to him.

"No. It's not my blood." He gives me a feral smile, and for some reason, I think this is hilarious. My laughter bounces off the walls.

He pulls me to my feet, and my dress flops off my shoulder, baring my breast. He's torn my gown, which makes me giggle again.

"I've got you," he murmurs and pulls me close. He lifts me off my feet, and I struggle until he tells me to stop.

"I'll hurt you." He's still recovering from getting shot, for godssakes.

"Elodie. Let me carry you."

I go very still so I don't hurt him. He hoists me against him, and I turn so I'm huddled against his chest, holding the scraps of my dress up so I'm not half topless.

"Now what?" The scent of smoke and incense is strong around us, making my head swim and think of rituals and vows uttered in Latin.

"Now we go home."

He starts walking through the dark. And despite every-thing—killing a man, getting fucked on the floor until my sex is sore and cum is running out of me—I feel warm all the way through.

He enters an elevator and speaks the code. *"Lasciate ogni speranza, voi ch'entrate."* The door closes, and the elevator ascends. I'll have to get him to teach me the code one day. But there'll be time for that.

We have forever.

EPILOGUE

J *aeger*

THERE'S nothing like springtime in the country. It wasn't so bad spending a long winter inside, hibernating on the couch with my *elita,* but it's nice to stand on the deck at the Lodge and breathe in the fresh air.

We came to Billionaire Island today, summoned by Damien. He likes to host what Lucy calls "family dinner." We used to gather like this on Sundays when we were kids, and Father Francis lured us into church by promising us a good meal. Now, we break bread by feasting on five courses, followed by expensive booze and cigars in the lounge.

I've left the festivities for a moment outside alone. Elodie's inside, hanging with a group of *elitas.* She's made friends, and I'm glad.

"Brother." Kaiser steps onto the deck. The forest scent hits him, and he inhales, tilting his head back. The fresh air washes the tension from his face. He sets his drink down on the railing and braces his hands on either side of it, gripping the wood and breathing deeply. His eyes are half-closed. I could tease him about communing with the trees or some shit, but I don't.

I say, "Did you ever think we would have something like this?"

His eyes blink open. Blue, like mine. Like looking into a mirror. Sometimes, I think I can hear his thoughts. They often mirror mine, too.

"No. But we had each other."

"We did. And now we have this." I smile at him, and his eyes crinkle. He doesn't smile, not like I do. But I'm looking past him into the Lodge, where Elodie sits in a cluster of women. She throws her head back, laughing.

"And you have her." Kaiser bumps my arm with his. I drag my eyes away from Elodie.

No one else can read Kaiser's stone expression, but I can. No one else would be able to hear the longing in his voice, but I do.

I know him as well as myself. He wants someone like my bunny. All the power and wealth mean nothing if there's no one to share midnights with.

That's why I forgave him so quickly for his betrayal. For a long time, he was all I had. It'll always be him and me, even though now it's him and me and her.

"St. James was looking for you," I say. "Maybe he has something for you." *Or someone.*

Kaiser grunts and glances back inside. I steal his drink and grin at him over the rim of the glass.

"Asshole," he says, but now even his lips are smiling.

"Hey, tomorrow night. Movie at our place. There's a new holiday rom-com."

"They're still playing those? It's not even Christmas."

"I bought them all for Elodie."

He snorts. "For Elodie. Sure."

"The long-lost prince has a brother." I waggle my brows.

"I'll bring the popcorn." He walks away, back inside, pausing to hold the door open for Elodie.

And then, it's just the two of us on the deck.

"There you are." Her cheeks are flushed, and her eyes are bright. She's found her footing in Fraternitas. Her ankle has long since healed, and she takes a few shifts at Inferno each week, waitressing while I sit at the bar to keep watch. And now, she knows almost everyone by name.

Today, she's luminous in a simple white dress and ballet flats. Her outfit reminds me of the first time we were at the Lodge together. I wonder if she wore white today on purpose.

I hold out my arm, and she comes to my side. I squeeze her close. There's a slight twinge in my gut near the scar of my bullet wound, but it's worth it. She leans into me, and I marvel at how right it feels.

She tilts her head, her collar flashing. "What are you doing out here?"

"It's nice out." I turn her so she's facing the forest.

"You like it out here. Would you ever want to move here?"

"Live on Billionaire Island?" It's not a leap of logic. All the Seven have homes here, plus St. James as well Damien, although few people know where his hidden mansion is. Unless you've done guard duty out there, which I have. "Naw. I like the penthouse."

"Me, too."

For a moment, we're still, watching the forest together.

Listening to the trill of the songbirds and the rustle of the leaves. Drinking in the peace.

She puts a hand on my chest and murmurs, "I have a gift for you."

"It's not my birthday."

"I know. It's mine." She slips something into my pocket and backs away, smiling. "If I run, will you chase me?"

"Always."

She kicks off her ballet flats, and my heartbeat shifts into a higher gear. My muscles tighten, but I force myself to be calm. To wait.

She pulls the pins out of her hair, and her curls come tumbling around her face.

"Give me a ten-minute head start, okay?"

I nod, unable to speak. There's a roaring waterfall in my head as my blood rushes, readying me for the hunt.

Elodie disappears down the stairs to the lawn. She walks to the treeline and stops to pull off her dress. The fading sunlight cups her curves, outlining her in gold. She's no longer human but otherworldly. A goddess of the forest.

Then she steps into the shadows and becomes real. She hangs the dress on the tree, smiles back at me, and slips into the woods.

I pull out the item she put in my pocket. It's a black hood with a skull painted on the front. Suddenly, I'm too hot.

But I wait. She gave me a fancy watch and a black turtleneck for Christmas after Kaiser and I had made fun of the big city fiancé's watch and clothes in one of the movies. I don't wear the turtleneck, but I like the watch. I half expected her to put "Big City Fiancé" on the back, but instead, she put "Big Bad Wolf" with a little heart, followed by "Bunny."

It's my second favorite gift, and I'll treasure it forever.

After ten minutes, I pull off the watch and put it on the railing. Kaiser will see it and make sure it gets back to me. If I wear it, it might get broken. I'm going to be careful and watch out for Elodie's ankle, and she'll hold back because of my gunshot wound, but still, things are going to get rough.

I pull off my shirt. The cool air hits my skin, but I'm still too hot. I wait until I'm about to enter the forest to pull on the hood. Before I do, I sniff the breeze. The scent of Elodie's arousal hangs in the air. I grab her dress and bring it to my face, inhaling it. So sweet. So excited and ready for me.

I drop the dress and pull on the hood. My world grows dark, my vision narrowing to the trail ahead. Finally, I lope into the forest to hunt, find, and claim my perfect prey.

KAISER

A GLINT of silver brings me out onto the deck again. Jaeger left his watch on the railing. I pick it up and pocket it. The woods are silent, betraying no secrets, but I know Jaeger's out there, hunting his *elita*.

I could stand out here and wish for things I don't have, or I can go inside and drink. So I head back inside. I walk right behind the bar and grab a whole bottle. The bartender only smiles at me. I almost wish he'd start something.

I need a good fight. I need to shed some blood and feel some pain. To know I'm alive.

The liquor burns, but it's not enough. If pain is going to be the only pleasure I have, I want more. A lot more.

But out here at the Lodge, I'm surrounded by Fraternitas. My found family. I don't want to fuck up anyone's happiness more than I already have. The last time I did that, Jaeger almost died.

I'm done with that.

I've always been the angry twin. I've had to be, to make sure my brother and I survived.

Jaeger doesn't hold onto things. He never has. He lets life roll off his back and finds his happiness where he can. He's like a hero in one of those fucking movies.

I'm glad he found happiness with her. But on days like today, it only serves to remind me there's no happiness to be had for someone like me.

"Kaiser." St. James is at my side. He's such a quiet fucker. Always has been. He was smaller than the rest of us as a boy. We protected him because some people are giants, even though they're small. And his intellect has saved us all.

"St. James." I lift the bottle in a mock toast. We have him to thank for all of this—the Lodge, the wealth, the power. But I'm not feeling grateful.

"Come with me to the library. I have something to show you."

"What?" I grunt, but I follow him to the room lined floor to ceiling with old books. I never come in here, but it's nice. I don't read, but I like the smell of leather and paper.

I set the bottle down on a side table. St. James drifts over and repositions the bottle on a coaster because he's civilized like that.

"I have something for you." He takes a square piece of paper out of his pocket and sets it on the table.

"What's this?" I ask without looking at it.

"A job."

I need a job. I need something to take my mind off everything.

The piece of paper is a photograph of a girl with a backpack, smiling shyly at the camera. Her hands are tight on the backpack straps like she's nervous, but there's a wistful light in her eyes.

Her face stops my heart. I've never seen her before, but I feel like I've known her forever.

Behind her is a sign that reads 'Unitas University.'

"What's the job?"

"Her."

Her. *Her.*

I stare at her face, barely hearing what St. James is saying.

"It'll be complicated, but that's why I need you. You can pull it off." He taps the photo, making sure I hear the next part. And I do. I hear it loud and clear.

"And when the job is done, there will be a reward."

Thank you for reading Elodie & Jaeger's story! Want to read about their first Christmas together? Check it out here: https://geni.us/HisPreyfreebie

Book 2 coming soon: https://geni.us/fraternitas02

Check out A Mafia Christmas Story here: https://geni.us/HisPreyfreebie

ALSO BY LEE SAVINO

For film and TV rights inquiries: <u>lee.savino@</u>
<u>leesavino.com</u>

Want more dark romance? Check out the **Dark Mafia Romance** trilogy written with Stasia Black. Start with Innocence.

Dark and Mafia Romance

Mafia Brides
Revenge is Sweet
Vengeance is Mine

Fraternitas
His Perfect Prey
His Perfect Possession

His Perfect Darkness
His Perfect Darkness
Darkest Before Dawn

A Dark Mafia Romance trilogy with Stasia Black
Innocence
Awakening
Queen of the Underworld

Beauty and the Rose trilogy with Stasia Black
Beauty's Beast
Beauty & the Thorns
Beauty & the Rose

~

Contemporary Romance

Royally Wrong
Royally Bad
Royally Fake Fiancé

Bad Boy Heroes
Her Marine Daddy
Her Dueling Daddies
Beauty & The Lumberjacks
Snowed in with the Lumberjack
Rescuing Regina

~

Paranormal romance

Berserker Saga
Sold to the Berserkers
Mated to the Berserkers
Bred by the Berserkers (FREE novella only available at
www.leesavino.com)
Taken by the Berserkers
Given to the Berserkers
Claimed by the Berserkers
Rescued by the Berserker

Captured by the Berserkers
Kidnapped by the Berserkers
Bonded to the Berserkers
Berserker Babies
Night of the Berserkers
Owned by the Berserkers
Tamed by the Berserkers
Mastered by the Berserkers
Surrendered to the Berserkers

Berserker Warriors
Aegir
Siebold with Ines Johnson

Bad Boy Alphas with Renee Rose
Alpha's Temptation
Alpha's Danger
Alpha's Prize
Alpha's Challenge
Alpha's Obsession
Alpha's Desire
Alpha's War
Alpha's Mission
Alpha's Bane
Alpha's Secret
Alpha's Prey
Alpha's Blood
Alpha's Sun

Shifter Ops with Renee Rose
Alpha's Moon
Alpha's Vow
Alpha's Revenge

Alpha's Fire
Alpha's Rescue
Alpha's Command

A Very Merry Alpha's Solstice

Bad Boy Bears with Renee Rose
Alpha's Claim

Midnight Doms with Renee Rose
Alpha's Blood
His Captive Mortal
The Virgin and the Vampire
(All Souls' Night anthology exclusive)

Werewolves of Wallstreet with Renee Rose
Big Bad Boss: Midnight
Big Bad Boss: Moon Mad
Big Bad Boss: Marked
Big Bad Boss: Mated

Sci fi romance

Planet of Kings with Tabitha Black
Brutal Mate
Brutal Claim
Brutal Capture
Brutal Beast
Brutal Demon

Tsenturion Warriors with Golden Angel

Alien Captive
Alien Tribute
Alien Abduction

Dragons in Exile with Lili Zander
Draekon Mate
Draekon Fire
Draekon Heart
Draekon Abduction
Draekon Destiny
Daughter of Draekons
Draekon Fever
Draekon Rogue
Draekon Holiday

Draekon Rebel Force with Lili Zander
Draekon Warrior
Draekon Conqueror
Draekon Pirate
Draekon Warlord
Draekon Guardian

Cowboy Romance

Rocky Mountain Mail Order Brides
Rocky Mountain Dawn
Rocky Mountain Bride
Rocky Mountain Rose
Rocky Mountain Romp
Rocky Mountain Rogue
Rocky Mountain Daddy

Rocky Mountain Ride
Possessing Pearl

Wild Whip Ranch with Tristan River
Cowboy's Babygirl
Taming His Wild Girl

ABOUT THE AUTHOR

USA today bestselling author Lee Savino has written over 69 steamy romance novels. Bad boys, mafia men, wolf shifters, and dragon shifters in space—her dominant, alpha-hole heroes will stop at nothing to possess their one true love. Happily-ever-after and book hangover guaranteed!

Download a free book at leesavino.com.

Connect with Lee Savino in her fabulous Goddess Group: https://www.facebook.com/groups/LeeSavino

Goodreads: http://bit.ly/2tqaH28
Bookbub: http://bit.ly/2h8N6le
TikTok: https://www.tiktok.com/@authorleesavino
Instagram: https://www.instagram.com/authorleesavino